with best wishes

4,

20
2006

NEVER TRY
TO HOLD A
RAINBOW

LLOYD DARVILL

Typeset and printed by Babash-Ryan Ltd
The Shadowline Building
Wembley Street
Gainsborough
Lincs. UK
DN21 2AJ

DEDICATED TO MY DEAR LATE WIFE VERA

CHAPTER 1

MONDAY THE 24TH OF APRIL started as most late April days do, with a fine, clear dawn around six o'clock. The difference however on this Monday, was that it was the end of the pregnancy for one of the women living in the back-to-back houses, and the day on which her fourth and last child would be born.

It had not been too bad a pregnancy, only that she had not wanted to be pregnant in the first place, as she felt that she was getting too old for child bearing. The thought of starting to bring up another child eight years after her last had never excited her from the start of her pregnancy.

The Great War had been won only a few years previously, and the country was just beginning to recover from its aftereffects. Bert, her husband had returned home safe and unharmed, unlike so many of her friends and neighbours. In the street where she lived, there had been those who had been killed, or many of those who did return came home wounded, limbless or mentally scarred. She had considered herself lucky that her husband came home, even though it was he who was responsible now for her being pregnant. During the nine months she had tried to force a miscarriage, but no such luck as she thought, and so on the 24th April, and on time, a baby boy was born.

The town, where this story starts in the early 1920s, did not possess a midwife, and so it was old Granny Andrews who helped bring the child into the world; within a few minutes the child was wiped, wrapped and given to the mother.

'There you are my dear, a beautiful day and a marvellous child to go with it. I shouldn't say beautiful, as that is what we say for girls and not for a boy, but he is a grand baby in every respect. You're very lucky in having such a grand little fellow, Mary.'

'Thank you very much for all your help Granny Andrews,

and I'm sure I'll love him now he is here,' said Mary (for that was the name of the new mother).

'It was you that helped yourself, I was only here to see you did it right my girl,' said Granny Andrews. 'You know Mary, I have helped deliver all your bairns, as well as many others in my time, and for some unknown reason this child seems to have made an impression on me more than any other has done. I can't say why, I just have a feeling that he is going to be special; well I suppose only time will tell. I won't be here to see or know of it when he is a grown man and made his way in life, if the Lord spares him from another war like we've just been through.'

Granny Andrews soon cleared up the things that had been used in the birth and once done said her goodbyes to Mary and her sister, who had now arrived to see the new baby and give any help that was required.

'How are you feeling Mary?' asked Eva.

Eva was older than Mary, and only had one child, a daughter who was in her early teens.

'I'm feeling sore down below,' answered Mary, 'and no wonder, after what I've just been through. This is definitely the last, and if our Bert wants any more he can have them himself!'

'Do you want a cup of tea Mary?' asked Eva.

'Not just now,' answered Mary, 'I think I'll just lie here quiet for a little while. Bring me the bairn, I'll suckle him then maybe he will fall asleep. I've always had plenty of milk before so I guess I will have for him as well.'

When the child had filled his little tummy he fell fast asleep. Mary just looked and smiled at him, as he lay so peaceful there in her arms. The birth had finally taken place when her other children had gone to school and Bert was at work. Eva did the washing, and what with the birth and the kids' and Bert's washing it seemed as if she was washing for the street. No wonder our Mary didn't want another bairn she thought, as she scrubbed the clothes against the scrubbing board. From washing to preparing the midday meal and running up and down the stairs to attend to Mary's few requests twelve 'o'clock soon arrived. Bert came home from work on his cycle, and was soon followed by the children who ran all the way home from school to see their new brother or sister.

'How is our Mary?' Bert asked Eva as he rushed in. 'Has she got anything yet?'

'Go and see for yourself,' said Eva, 'and don't be long, as your dinner is almost ready, and the kids'll be here soon, and our Ann's coming.'

Ann was Eva's daughter, and being an only child was more spoilt than Mary's children. Eva's husband Tom was a sailor on the continental sea trips and was rarely at home, so Eva had always let Ann have anything she wanted to compensate for not often having her father around.

This family lived in a small town that had grown over the last hundred years around an inland seaport. Most of the inhabitants of the town derived their livelihood from working at the shipyard either building ships or dealing with incoming and outgoing cargo.

After a day or so, Mary was back up looking after the family and the new baby. There was still the usual cleaning, cooking, washing and other chores as well as all the extra work that a newborn baby made, therefore it was not surprising that she went to bed exhausted every night. Eva often came round to see Mary, but more for a chat and a cup of tea than to help her sister in any way, even though she had more time on her hands.

Bert was a good man and had made Mary a good husband. Although he enjoyed a drink, like most of the local chaps who had returned from the war, he had never came home drunk or wasted all his money on alcohol. He had also never laid a finger on her, not that she had deserved to be hit or shouted at. Many of the women who lived in the streets near Mary were not as fortunate in their husbands and had accepted that their lives were about bringing up children, looking after the house, living with no money and being beaten by drunken husbands. Little changed in the lives of the occupants of these back-to-back houses; this was the way in which things had always seemed to be and always would.

The summer soon came and went, and all too soon November with its colder days and even colder nights came. Darkness would begin to creep in by around four 'o'clock and the gas lighter would come round with his long lit pole and light the few lamps in the town. It was not the most rewarding of jobs and the pay wasn't good, but at least it was a job, and in the days that were to follow this and the money would mean a lot.

Mary had two older sons, one eight and the other twelve; her first child a girl had tragically been stillborn. Her two older sons were different in most ways: size, temperament and looks. As in most cases with brothers, they did not always agree, and the four years did make up quite a difference. As of yet, the arrival of the new baby had not made a great deal of change to their lives: the food was on the table as usual, their clothes were still washed and ironed and their beds were always made. Their home was clean and tidy; their mum never seemed to have much time on her hands before the new baby came, so to them it was life as usual. Their dad was off to work before they awoke every morning, they would have breakfast, go to school, come home for lunch, back to school, and then would be home again by four 'o'clock. They would then go out and play and do the usual activities that boys of their age got up to: keeping themselves and their clothes clean was not one of them. They were no better or worse than any of the kids in their street.

The streets around where they lived were all the same, rows of small back-to-back terraced homes that is if they could be called 'homes', as most had more people in the family than there were rooms in the house. At the top of the street, where Mary and her family lived, was the local school that both her elder sons went to. Built at the end of the last century, the school was divided with the girls on one side of the building and the boys on the other. A brick wall, six feet high divided the schoolyard, which kept the boys apart from the girls during school hours. The entrance to the boys' schoolrooms was on the street where Mary and her family lived; the girls' schoolrooms were entered from the next street. Quite a number of streets and roads made up the area that the school catered for. Most, if not all of the streets had a corner shop, a butcher, baker, grocer, fried fish and chip shop or cobbler, each and every one helping to create the local community and earn a living.

It was a visit to the corner grocer's shop that Mary's middle son was sent to on one memorable occasion, his name was Herbert Alfred, but was generally called Alfred by his family so as not to confuse him with his father.

'Go and buy me a packet of salt, Alfred, and take the baby in the pram with you,' asked Mary.

'Can't William go?' replied Alfred, (William being the older brother). 'He'll be quicker than me, he's larger and his legs are longer.'

'I told you to go, not William, so off you go. Here's the money, put it in your pocket and don't lose it....and don't be long. David's in his pram and is fast asleep, so don't wake him as I have only just got him off to sleep after his feed.'

After a scowl and a grin Alfred put the coin in his pocket. He walked into the back yard to where the pram was standing, looked at the sleeping baby and puckered up his face and stuck out his tongue at his brother. He took the brake off the pram and walked down the garden path, through the back gate and along the narrow back lane. The back lane had only been covered with concrete a few months previously so it was easy to push and manoeuvre the pram. At the end of the back lane he turned right, walked on for a hundred yards until he came to the grocer's shop. The time was about a quarter past four as on this day he had come straight home from school, which was unusual for him as normally he sauntered home, but today he had been hungry and the thought of food at home had speeded him up. Before he could tell her of his hunger, Mary had said that there was no tea ready as she needed salt for the meal and had told him to go to the shop to buy some. He parked the pram in front of the shop, put on the brake and went inside.

'Bag of salt please,' he asked.

Mr Brown, the grocer looked amazed at Alfred, he could hardly believe his ears, here was one of the local boys in his shop saying "please". As he served Alfred and gave him his change, he remarked, 'I see you have brought your baby brother with you. I bet you're proud to have a young man like him for your little brother, hey? He is such a fine little fellow; I wish I had one like him.'

'I'll swap him for a bar of chocolate if you like and I'll throw in the pram,' said Alfred.

'Get on with you,' said the shopkeeper, 'whatever would your mum say?'

Alfred picked up the salt, put the change in his pocket and turned to leave the shop when he bumped into one of his playmates, John from the next street, who had just entered the shop.

'Hi Alf,' said John, 'care for a game of football? I've got a ball'.

From his pocket he produced a battered old tennis ball. 'Don't you dare bounce that ball in this shop,' said Mr Brown fearing for his stock and his windows.

'Old misery,' said John under his breath as he left the shop.

'OK,' said Alfred, as he stuffed the bag of salt into his pocket and made off down the street chasing after his friend.

They proceeded to kick the ball between them and Alfred completely forgot that he had left his baby brother David fast asleep outside the shop in his pram.

It's surprising how fast time goes when two lads have a ball to kick about, and twenty past four when Alfred set off for the salt soon became five 'o'clock. It was then that Alfred felt the salt in his pocket and remembered that his mum would be waiting at home for it. Kicking the ball past his mate he shouted, 'So long, see you later,' and ran home as fast as he could, through the back gate down the path and into the kitchen.

'Wherever have you been and where is our David?' asked Mary.

Alfred did not stop to answer or to empty his pocket of the packet of salt. When he had run home, he had run fast, but not as fast as he ran back to the grocery shop. To his dismay the pram with David in had disappeared. His heart sank to his boots until he saw through the window that the pram was safe inside the shop.

'Want to swap him for a bar of chocolate?' said Mr Brown, picking up a bar of chocolate.

'No thanks Mister,' said Alfred pushing the pram through the shop door, much to the delight of Mrs Brown who had joined her husband from the back of the shop.

'As time goes by, that kid may have one or two looks of relief on his face in the future, but I dare say none more so than just now when he saw the pram and his baby brother in our shop,' said Mrs Brown.

By the time that Alfred, David and the pram were back home, Bert was home from work, and William was sat at the table waiting for his tea. Bert was washing his hands at the sink in the kitchen, and couldn't help hearing what Mary was saying to Alfred.

'And where did you find our David then? I'll bet that you left him outside the shop and forgot him didn't you? I dare say you were kicking your shoes out as usual, anyone 'ud think new shoes grew on trees.'

'I promise, I promise, I won't ever forget him again Mum,' stammered Alfred.

'Like hell you won't,' said Bert coming from the kitchen unbuckling his belt, 'I reckon some of this belt will help you remember my lad.'

'No dad, no dad,' wailed Alfred.

'Don't you lay a finger on him,' shouted Mary, 'can't you see that he's scared enough without any more hurt, there is enough pain, hurt and sorrow in these streets without you adding to it. I'll not have it here in my house, do you hear?'

Bert fastened his belt back up, but the look he gave to Alfred hurt as much, if not more than the belt would have done.

'And it's bed for you as soon as you have had your tea,' answered Bert, 'there's no going out to play tonight my lad.'

That night as Mary lay in Bert's arms in bed she said, 'You know Bert, I'll bet our Alfred was scared when he realised what he had done, leaving our David as he did. He really does love our David and I'm sure David loves him too. Have you seen the way his eyes follow Alfred's every movement? He may always be complaining that all he does is cry and fill his nappy, but he does care for him.'

They both had a little chuckle together. 'I do love you so much you know Mary,' he said as he kissed her goodnight in the darkness of the bedroom.

CHAPTER 2

SPRING CHANGED TO SUMMER, and it was surprising how quickly four years had passed since the birth of David. William was now 16 years old, Alfred twelve and David a sturdy four year old. Mary, too, was also four years older, and at times she knew and felt it. Life was not easy for such women as Mary in the neighbourhood where she lived. A chore, such as washing clothes on family washday, was really hard labour. She would have to bring fuel into the kitchen to heat the water and then pour it into the peggy tub, then rub the clothes hard against the scrubbing board in order to get the soiled clothes clean. This often took a lot of time and effort as Bert's uniform that he wore down on the docks was always black with dirt, and even the children managed to get their clothes filthy playing out on the streets.

Life was not getting any easier; unemployment was getting worse in the area with more men being laid off work each week. So far Bert had managed to hold onto his job, but for how long no one knew; this was the start of hard times to come with more to follow. In the town in which they lived many people's livelihoods relied on the sea: the ships and their trade to Europe. Even in Bert's street, from number 29 to about number 65, the male members of the families worked long, hard hours on the docks, railways or in the shipyard.

Up until recently the town had always been fairly prosperous, the Great War had meant that there had always been a demand for maintaining war work and building ships but within the last year things in the town had taken a change, and not for the better. The miners had gone on strike for more pay and so there had been no coal production, which meant that there was no coal or coke to transfer by rail or sea out of the town. A tariff on goods leaving and entering the country had been introduced, when this happened it seemed to be the last nail in the coffin for this seaport. It was not long before the contracts for any new ships which were to be built there were cancelled, those ships that were due to be repaired were cancelled and the whole of the shipyard was closed down, except for a very few men who were retained for maintenance work.

When Bert came home that Saturday lunchtime and Mary saw the look on his face, she knew the worst and felt as though someone had struck her a blow in the stomach.

'Well that's it Mary, I'm now on the dole. I'm out of work now along with many more, and now that the war is over I guess even the army wouldn't want me.'

'Don't talk like that,' said Mary trying to put on a brave face, 'we will manage somehow, it won't be easy, but we will survive. At least you came back from the war, for that I shall be eternally grateful. Come on get your dinner before it gets cold.'

With it being a Saturday Alfred was not at school and had heard what his father had said regarding losing his job. William was at work and, of course, David, who had not started school, was playing on the floor with a toy. During their meal everyone sat in awkward silence, even young David seemed to know and kept quiet at the table eating his meat without any fuss. William, who worked till lunchtime on a Saturday, soon returned home, and as he entered the room said to his father, 'Is it true then Dad, has the yard closed from today?'

'Yes lad, it's true,' replied Bert, 'I don't know when the shipyard will open again, but my guess is that it could take years.'

'Don't say that Bert,' said Mary.

'I hope I'm wrong, but only time will tell,' said Bert pushing his empty plate to one side. He picked David up from his high chair, 'Come on my bonny wee bairn, let's have you for a minute,' he said as he sat down in his armchair with David on his knee. David ran his hands through his Dad's hair gurgled and laughed as he and his Dad made funny faces at one another. Bert loved his family and the thought of dark days to come filled him with fear, although he tried hard not to show it to Mary and the kids as he played with David.

When the meal was finished and Mary had washed the dishes and put things away, for she was a very neat and particular person as all the street knew, she said, 'I think I'll have a walk to see my sister, I'll be back before teatime. Look after David for me; it'll make a change for me. I have a wee bit of shopping to do and I can do it as I go and see her.'

'Alright,' said Bert, 'give her and that stuck up daughter of hers my regards,' and laughed as he said it.

Mary soon washed and changed into her going out clothes and when she was ready to leave the house, she came over to where Bert and David were sitting. Bert was reading a storybook to David, who appeared very interested in the story that Bert was telling him. Mary bent over, gave them both a kiss and said, 'I shan't be too long, cheerio for now.'

Mary looked neat and tidy; she was tall in stature, had a thin figure, a good bone structure and a good complexion, all in all she was a good looking woman for her years, especially considering that she had had four children.

As she walked up the street on her way to the town and her sister's, she was acknowledged by one or two of her neighbours, who were standing talking at their doors.

'Hello Mary, going somewhere nice?' they asked her.

'I am,' answered Mary, refusing to answer where she was going. That will keep them guessing she chuckled to herself. She was not a spiteful or devious person, in fact Mary was quite the opposite, which was why she was held in such high esteem by all who knew and came into contact with her.

When she reached the town she bought the shopping that she required, and gazed longingly at goods that she knew she could no longer afford, for the dole would not go as far as a weekly wage. When Bert had been in the army, they only had a small allowance to live on, but in those days the family was smaller: there were only two children to clothe and feed and no Bert to provide for. Now she had two children, a hungry man and a growing lad called David to provide for and feed. As Mary walked on down the High Street, she spoke and smiled to each and every person she met and knew. The last shop window she looked in was a jewellers, and over the door hung three golden balls to advertise that it was a pawnbroker as well. Mary had a quick glance at the jewellery on display in the window, turned and proceeded on her way.

The shop was owned by a Mr Levine and his wife who had come to England from Russia a few years ago. They had settled in the town and had been accepted and welcomed into the local community from the start. Mr and Mrs Levine had one child, a daughter, a year or so older than David. Mrs Levine had had her late on in life, which had been a surprise for both her and her husband, as well as for the local community.

It was not a great distance from Mr Levine's shop to Eva's, and Mary quite enjoyed the walk in the fresh air. Knocking on the door, which was quickly opened by Eva's daughter Ann, who said, 'Come in Aunt Mary, nice to see you. I haven't seen you for quite some time. I have no excuse except that I have been busy as usual, and time does seem to go quick these days.'

'Yes it does,' answered Mary. She thought to herself, I guess our Ann is getting more pleasant and sociable as she gets older, and she was.

'Sit down,' said Ann, 'Mum won't be long, she's just popped out, I'll make you a cup of tea.' Mary sat down and by the time the cup of tea arrived Eva had returned.

'Hello Mary, how are you and your brood keeping?'

'Not too bad,' answered Mary, 'guess we have a lot to be thankful for.'

After an hour or so had passed and they had discussed the local gossip Mary said her goodbyes, and proceeded on her way home. She took the longest way home. The sun shone, the air was warm, the sky high, all in all, it was a perfect day. What a pity the world was not as good as the day, thought

Mary as she walked on home, and although she didn't realise it at that moment, within a few years the whole world would have altered, never to be the same again.

The next few months seemed to go somewhat quicker than usual, maybe that was because she found more work to do: repairing clothes, turning collars and cuffs on shirts and sewing patches on trousers. Now that the housekeeping was dependent on the dole pay, anything that she could save had to be considered. It was the same in most houses up and down the street, where the women had to bear the worst of these harsh times. In reality it was no doubt more of a hardship for the men having no work to do. Small groups began to congregate on street corners to talk and complain to each other about anything and everything, looking and feeling worse with each and everyday.

Bert had an allotment not too far from home that he had rented since he had been demobbed from the army, and it was there that he passed away most of his time. Bert grew most of their vegetables on the allotment and in this respect Mary and her family were lucky. Mary was more than a good housekeeper in all areas of the housework, and Bert was more than happy having her as his wife.

Christmas came and went, as did the next few Christmases. No work opportunities arose for most of the men in the town. New babies were born, older folk passed away and life's pattern continued its cycle. It became increasingly difficult for parents of these families to feed and sleep children as they grew up into adults. It had been easy when they were small: they could share baths and washing facilities, but as they grew up they respected each other's privacy, and as soon as they could afford to, some left home when they had a job. In Mary's case having just boys was not too bad for sleeping arrangements.

With Bert having the allotment and growing a lot of vegetables it certainly helped a lot, and no one was more appreciative of it than Mary, who made good use of them. If she ever had any spare she always gave them away to her friends and neighbours. In these dire days everyone helped one another when they could.

In the summer, when needed, Bert helped a small-time farmer on odd occasions and was paid in kind. One day when the farmer and Bert were looking in the pigsty at the sow and her litter, the farmer remarked, 'what a nice litter of pigs they are, except for that one who has not grown like the others.'

Being small and weak, it had been deprived of milk due to being pushed away at feeding time by the others who were larger and stronger. 'I think I'll have to destroy the weak one, and do it a favour,' said the farmer.

'Please may I have it?' asked Bert.

'You have it, where will you house it?' asked the farmer. 'You have no sty.'

'I have an allotment,' replied Bert, 'and I'll build a sty. I'm sure one or two of my friends will help me.'

'I dare say it will save me a job digging a hole to bury it Bert, so if you want it take it. I'll find a potato sack for you to put it in, and I'll be pleased to see the back of it.'

They found a sack, parted the mother pig from the litter and after a hectic quarter of an hour of sweat, swearing and the squealing of the pigs, they managed to corner the small pig and put it into the sack for Bert to take away.

As Bert left, the farmer remarked, 'Where are you going to keep it tonight? You can't tie it to the table with its hind-leg, and I don't suppose your Mary will want to share her bed with it, bad enough you snoring without a pig also.'

'I know where it will sleep tonight,' remarked Bert, 'so I'll have some of these bedclothes please,' stuffing one or two handfuls of clean straw on to the pig in the sack. It gave a squeal as Bert threw the sack over his shoulder and said goodbye to the farmer.

When he arrived home, Bert soon paid a visit to one of his near neighbours who had a large dog kennel, which was not in use as the old dog had died a few weeks ago. Knocking on the door, he asked if his friend was in, and could he have a word with him. When his friend arrived he smiled, and asked Bert if he could be of help, and when Bert requested the loan of the dog kennel he burst out laughing.

'Are you getting a dog Bert? You always said you would never have a dog.' He laughed even more so when told it was to house a pig and not a dog.

'It can't be a very large pig Bert, as our old dog never seemed to have too much room in it, and always used to stretch when he came out.'

'It will only be for a little while as I intend to build a sty in the next few days down on the allotment.'

'Of course you can have it.'

'I promise I'll return it clean,' said Bert and left.

After borrowing a handcart from one of the local tradesmen, he proceeded to take the dog kennel home. After putting the straw in he took the pig out of the sack and introduced it to its new home, and then attached a piece of wire netting over the entrance to keep it in. He returned the handcart and went in doors to wash his hands and arms. When he told Mary and the boys of his prize they were not as enthusiastic as him, and even much less when they saw the size of the animal.

'Percy Jackson down the street has a guinea pig bigger than that,' said Alfred.

Bert smiled and replied, 'Maybe he has, but Percy's pig has stopped growing now, but my pig has yet to grow.'

Young David was more impressed than the rest of the family and promised to help care for its welfare. Bert made a sty in the next few days and when the pig was transferred from the kennel to the sty it looked smaller than ever, and even Bert wondered if he had done the right thing in bringing it down from the farm. David kept his promise to help care for Betsy: Betsy being the name he had given the pig. Their neighbours and friends saved potato peelings and food scraps for Betsy that David collected every day in his 'pig bucket' as he called it.

The small pig ate all the food that she was given but never seemed to grow. Then all at once she changed, a curl appeared in her tail, the wrinkles went and she grew out of all recognition in a matter of weeks. David seemed to be as pleased as Bert in the change in the animal, and even more so when he was told that the change in Betsy was due to the attention that he had given her.

David, like Betsy was growing fast, he was a big boy for his age, and unlike William and Alfred, seemed quieter and more solitary. He did not seek the company of the other children and never wanted to join them down the street to play games. David was growing up, he was cheerful, pleasant and clean, too clean an appearance for some of the other local kids who got far more grubby than he, but for this Mary did not mind and often spoke of this to Bert when they were alone and were discussing things in general.

'He is alright,' said Bert, 'it's nice to have a quiet one around. He thinks a lot, does our David, but doesn't always say what he's thinking, which sometimes is not a bad thing. Sometimes it's better to stop and think first, and that's what he usually does. When we are together I think he is growing up too fast. Only the other day he said that when Betsy is large enough and goes away he will miss her, but he understands that the reason we had her in the first place was so that she would feed us. He said, "I won't cry, I only hope I'm at school when they take her away, and I dare say you'll feel the same as me Dad, as you and I have looked after her more while she has been here, and maybe when we have a little more money you will buy another pig for us to take care of."'

Mary and Bert were good parents and had kept the family together with love and affection through these hard and difficult years.

William had recently applied for a job in London, as job prospects and money were more available there. He was more than delighted when the post arrived one morning saying that he had been offered the position, but Mary was not so happy. The thought of him leaving home and the district, even if he was now a fully-grown man, filled her with apprehension.

'Don't worry,' said Bert, 'our William is a fully-grown man now, it's time he left home. It'll make him realise how much you've done for him, and still do for that matter.'

Mary did not think as Bert did, and that was the difference between mother and father. When the day came for William to go to London and his new job, Mary was like a mother hen with a brood of chicks. She and the family had never been parted before, and even though William was a man now she still considered him as one of her 'bairns'.

The time to catch the train came all too soon. William had said his goodbyes to Alfred at breakfast, and to David before he went to school. As Mary stood in the passage leading to the front door, William put his arms around her and almost squeezed the breath out of her, gave her a big kiss and said, 'You are still my favourite girlfriend Mum.'

'Go on with you,' said Mary, wiping away a tear, 'take care, write to us soon please.'

With that they parted and she waved goodbye. Bert and William walked down the street to the railway station, and the two of them seemed to talk more freely than they had ever done. As they shook hands as William boarded the train, both were filled with emotion, though neither dared showed it in front of the other.

As Bert walked home he did not hurry, but his thoughts went back to his own departure from home some years before, but his train ride then was not a journey to London but a journey to the army and the war. His mind went back to his own terrifying experiences of what he had seen and lived through, and he hoped that none of his sons would have to serve their King and country as he had done. He had been told then that he was fighting for a better world and prosperity; but unemployment, bad housing and poor food made him wonder what he had given almost four years of his life for. These thoughts soon disappeared as a short shower of light rain came and he quickened his step to a shop doorway to shelter. As he looked at the goods on display in the window he thought to himself, 'I wish I could take that dress for my Mary, I bet she'd look lovely in it. Ah well, maybe one day, but not today,' he sighed, as he turned the small amount of coins over in his trouser pockets. The rain had eased and he stepped out into the street and made his way home. Bert didn't choose to spend much time talking to the gangs of unemployed men who regularly stood on street corners. He preferred to spend much of his time on his own in the small garden shed on his allotment. In many ways David took after his Dad, for Bert was a loner in that respect.

When Bert arrived home for dinner, he was the last to sit down at the table. Mary and the boys had already started their meal. Mary got up and took a plate out of the oven and put it down in front of her husband.

'Don't blame me if your dinner is spoilt and not too hot, I have kept it as warm as I could,' she said.

'It will be ok,' said Bert, 'I'll not complain.'

'Won't do you any good,' said Mary with a smile, 'time is time in this house as you should know by now.'

Mary was more than lucky having Bert for a husband, as quite a few of her neighbours would have been nursing a swollen face right now if they had said that to their husbands. Most times Bert took her banter in good nature. From then the meal was eaten in silence; William's departure was soon taking effect on them all.

CHAPTER 3

WILLIAM KEPT HIS PROMISE to his Mum regarding writing home.
Mary couldn't wait for his first letter to arrive, and after
reading it felt more at ease with herself. His letters were
always very informative and interesting. He wrote of the work
he was doing, how busy London was in comparison to his
home; he described the people, the way of life, and to her it
was as if she were there with him. She always answered his
letters with all the family news and local gossip, and at least
she knew by the letters he sent that he was happy and had
settled into his new life, which helped put her mind at rest.

Life at home did not change a great deal. Day by day, month
by month another year slipped quickly by. There had been
rumours that the shipyard was to reopen and that work on
the docks would restart in the near future, but as of yet they
were still rumours.

When the time came for the demise of Betsy the pig, David
was at school and had not been told that it was going to
happen, even though he had been warned that her departure
from this world was to be in the near future. Eva came to help
Mary utilise all the by-products from Betsy, and all of the
neighbours and friends were more than thankful for all that
Mary offered to them. After the deed was done and David
had learnt of it he helped Bert clean and wash out the sty.

Bert said to David as they worked, 'Maybe one day we
will have two pigs, if and when we are richer than we are
today, and then they can keep each other company,' and
smiled as he pulled David towards him for a hug.

Now that Betsy had gone, David seemed to have more time
on his hands. When off school and at weekends, he spent quite
a lot of his spare time at the allotment, and seemed more at
ease in the company of the older men tending their vegetable
plots than with the girls and boys of his own age who played
games in the streets near their homes. One of the older men
at the allotments commented to Bert that David, 'Has too old

a head on his shoulders for a child of his age, he's always asking questions, but I'll say that he is never cheeky. He's always polite and shows an interest in things that we are doing and how we do them, how much we spend on seed, how long they take to grow and most of all how much would they have cost in the shops.'

'Don't learn if you don't ask,' replied Bert, 'and our David is interested in some things more than others, mores the pity.'

As David and Bert were walking home they seemed to the public more like a couple of middle-aged men than a father and younger son. If they stopped to speak to a friend or neighbour, David always kept in the background and never tried to interfere or join in the conversation.

Thanks to his parents teaching he certainly knew his manners and it certainly showed and was much appreciated. On this occasion they seemed to meet very few whom they knew so were able to enter into more conversation with one another as they walked along.

'You know Dad what I would like,' said David, 'although I know I won't get it.'

'What would you like?' replied Bert.

David waited a moment or so before replying, and then in a subdued voice said, 'A wheelbarrow, but not a garden or a kid's wheelbarrow, after tea I'll draw what I mean on a piece of paper. I know where I can get some wheels for it. When I was passing Mrs Taylor talking to Mrs Jones I overheard her say that now her youngest is walking, she is going to get rid of her pram, and she would give it away to anyone. I asked if I could have it. She said, "you're a bit large to ride in a pram aren't you, and I should say a bit young to want to start a family of your own". They both burst out laughing but eventually said that I could have it. "What do you want it for, a trolley I guess?" she asked. I told her I wanted to make a wheelbarrow from it, well when I say wheelbarrow, I meant a cross between a handcart and a wheelbarrow. "Well it will be a change to it ending up as a trolley I guess," she answered, "as most of the children want to make four wheel trolleys out of them so that they can ride and steer them up and down the street".'

'What do you want a wheelbarrow for?' asked Bert.

'When I've drawn you a picture of what I want, I'm sure you'll see and understand what I mean Dad.'

As they were almost home their conversation drew to a close. As they entered the house they smiled and they were greeted with the usual smile from Mary.

'I guess your stomach is a better time keeper than a watch in your pocket,' she said, 'well at least you're on time today, so for now I'll not complain.'

'We're always on time, and you're always complaining,' answered Bert sarcastically.

'Get your tea, that's enough cheek for now,' she said as she sat down to join them for their meal.

Alfred had said that he would be late for his tea, and so the three of them sat there in semi-silence. When the meal had been eaten, the table cleared and the dishes washed and cleared away, Mary picked up some of her knitting, Bert read the paper and David proceeded to sketch his wheelbarrow come handcart. He had previously looked at the butcher's and greengrocer's handcarts and the railway porter's wheelbarrow on the station platform with its large steel hoop on the end, and he knew that he wanted to design a mixture of both. When David had finished the sketch of his cart he took it to his father, who had now finished reading his paper.

'It looks an odd sort of an object to me David, do you think it will work?'

'I hope so,' answered David, 'I know it has not got any springs like a handcart which the tradesmen use, but the barrows that the station porters use do not have springs either. I have found the wheels from Mrs Taylor's pram, they are good strong wheels but I know we can't find any springs to go with the wheels, so my design is a cross between the two.

I'm sure it will work, will you help me to make it?'

'Course I will, but what do you want with a cart so large, and where are you going to store it?'

'Honest Dad, it won't be any larger than a porter's barrow, maybe just a wee bit wider, and the pram wheels being larger than those on the barrow should make it easier to push. If we stand it on its end, I'm sure it won't take up too much room at the end of the backyard, or at the allotment, and if we can make a good job of it I'll tell you then what I want it for.'

'Alright,' said Bert, 'I will keep an eye open for any old bits of timber or nails and we'll have a go at making one. Don't lose the plans and blueprints that you have just drawn up.'

'Thanks Dad,' he said and ran upstairs.

Bert gave a half smile to Mary, and she smiled back at him as she proceeded with her knitting.

Not many days had passed before David paid a visit to Mrs Taylor's for the pram. Having collected it he pushed it home feeling proud in the knowledge that he was the owner of four good wheels, and hopefully soon a good strong barrow. Over the next few days Bert, along with some of his friends, made a start on David's barrow down at the allotments. They used any spare bits of wood and metal that they could find without any cost to themselves. One of Bert's friends was a shipwright, so the wood was planed smooth and measured correctly; another was a blacksmith who used his blowtorch to shape the iron and steel hoops and fitments. When the job was completed, someone found enough paint from a leftover paint job to make it very smart and presentable. Bert thanked his old workmates for their help, and as they departed to their own plots on the allotment he remarked, 'Soon we will be building ships again, instead of contraptions like this, pointing to the barrow'.

What the men on the allotments didn't realise was that many of them would soon be back in employment, even though England had not yet cast off her own dark days after the Great War and the stock market crash. Across Europe, dictators were causing unrest in Germany, Spain and Italy, and would soon threaten the stability of the continent. Employment would soon mean the army – fighting for king and country against fascism.

When David came home from school at four 'o'clock he went straight to where Bert and his pals were, as he knew that his request had been granted and his barrow completed. When he saw it his eyes lit up, his face gave a huge smile as it was just as he had envisaged it to be, only bigger and stronger than he could have hoped for.

'Thank you ever so much Dad, its fantastic, its great.'

'Go thank those chaps over there,' said Bert, 'for they helped me make it as much as I did.'

When David had been and thanked each of the men for helping his Dad, David and Bert realised it was almost teatime, and so made their way home. David could not wait to get home to show Mary his prize new possession. Even the old wheels looked better for the coat of paint, as did the rest of the wood and steel.

When Mary saw it she asked, 'Why do you want something so workman-like in appearance?'

David replied, 'I hope that it will provide me with a job in the near future.'

And that was his only answer, or at least all he said for the time being. Not wanting to pry too much into his business, Mary and Bert decided to wait and see what he had in mind for the near future. When Alfred came home later and saw David's new acquisition propped up in the back yard he burst out laughing as he entered the house.

'Wherever did that contraption come from, and whoever owns it?' he asked.

'Its mine,' beamed David, 'Dad and his pals made it for me, isn't it great?'

'If you say so our kid,' for "our kid" was how Alfred

often referred to his younger brother, 'but I bet that all the other kids would sooner have had a trolley than that object.'

'Well I'm not like all the other kids, am I?' answered David, 'and its not an object so there.'

When they had finished their evening meal, which they had all seemed to enjoy, and before the dishes were cleared away, Mary said, 'I had a letter from our William today and in it he asked if I would like to pay him a visit in London and stay with him in his lodgings for a few days. His landlady has a spare room for me to stay in; he has saved up some money and will send me the train fare. I have never been as far as London. All day I have had it going round in my head, I can't go, I can go, so whatever you three say I'll abide by your decision either way, so there I've said my piece.'

Alfred was the first to answer, 'I say go if our William has been good enough to save up his money to give you a break, and in London. I say take it, don't throw the kindness back in his face, if ever anyone deserved a break you do, the way you have cared for us in these hard years, you deserve it, go.'

'I guess our Alfred has answered for us, hasn't he David?' said Bert, 'but after my cooking and house keeping, I reckon we'll be pleased to see her return to us.'

Mary had hoped against hope that that would be their answer, as she really wanted to see London, and of course William, that was only natural. She soon replied to William saying that the family had agreed and that she would love to go and stay with him. The days that followed were more than hectic for Mary, what with extra washing, cleaning and baking. Her days were busy indeed and when bedtime came, sleep soon followed as she laid her head on the pillow.

On Fridays and Saturdays the town centre shops and market bustled with custom. David had noticed how busy all the market stalls were, and that they never seemed to have enough staff, even though unemployment was still rife. One particular Saturday, when there was a lull in the trade, which was unusual, David walked up to one of the stallholders and in quite business like tones enquired if he could help out in any way. The person to whom he was speaking looked David up and down for a moment and then said, 'You help? Can you skin a rabbit, or a fish, or serve the customers?'

'No sir,' answered David, 'but I can clear all those empty cases that hold onions and oranges. I have my own barrow to move them away, I know you fetch many of your rabbits from the station and I could fetch you some cases on my barrow, it is strong enough and so am I, you see I can lift a case of rabbits.'

As there was one nearby he obliged by picking up the case of about a dozen and a half rabbits that were in their skins but disembowelled. 'If I can have the empty cases from the oranges and onions I will have that as payment for my work, and if I don't come up to your expectations just tell me so and I won't pester you again sir.'

It was the business like manner of the youngster and the fact that he had been called 'sir' that impressed the stallholder most of all. 'Alright,' said the man, 'I'll give you a try, when can you start?'

'As soon as I get my barrow,' said David. 'Thank you sir,' and with that he was on his way.

He arrived home to collect the barrow, he told his mother that he would be back for lunch, and then left the house. When he returned to the market, he set about clearing the empty cases, and with a small hammer, which he had brought from home, soon knocked the sides and dividing sections off, taking care not to split or break the wood more than was necessary, before placing each in a neat pile, out of harms way. He found a sweeping brush and shovel and swept up. David returned after lunch, and after a visit to the railway station to enquire about extra rabbits that had not arrived, he continued his tidying up of the extra cases and vegetable remains that were lying around the market stall. The men behind the stall remarked to each other about the efficient way David was working. When it came for him to finish work there, he parcelled up all his pieces of packing cases, which he had put carefully into piles, and placed them on his barrow. As he was leaving he asked the man if his work had been satisfactory and would they like him to return next weekend?

'OK,' replied the stallholder, 'here you are young'un,' and he placed a sixpence in David's hand. 'Don't spend it all at once and don't expect it every time you come.'

David could hardly thank the man enough, as he looked at the money in his hand. The stallholder was more than pleased to think that the cases had been got rid of and that the back of his stall was tidy. David put the sixpence safely in his pocket, picked up the handles of his barrow, and proceeded to push his wood home; he was more than ready for his next meal as the hard work and fresh air had made him hungry.

When Mary and Bert inquired what he had been up to all day, he remarked, 'Busy I guess,' and that was the only answer he gave. In response he asked them if they too had had a good day and what they had been up to. Later when Bert saw the wood in the yard he enquired where it had come from. When David told him, Bert said 'What are you going to do with it?'

David gave a small grin, 'Sell it I hope,' and disappeared from the house into the yard.

Finding a pair of pincers he set about removing all the nails from the wood, and there were many to be removed. Making sure that he didn't bend any nails in their extraction - and any he did bend he tried to straighten - he then placed them in the small tin he had found. He continued to build up his supply of wood and nails over the next few weeks as he regularly went to the market on Friday evenings when he had finished school and all day Saturday.

One Friday his hands were very sore and he was in pain. During the afternoon lesson David was not paying attention to the teacher, who was of the old school and a stickler for discipline.

'Repeat what I have just said, Jones,' yelled Mr Thomas.

David who had been wondering how many cases would be at the market, could not repeat the question Mr Thomas had asked.

'You are a dreamer, my boy. Come out here, I'll wake you from your dreams; dreams won't earn you a living. Hold out your hands.'

David did as he was told and held both his hands out, palms uppermost, where upon he received three hard strokes from a thin cane on each. He returned to his seat nursing two very sore hands.

As David and one of his classmates were leaving the school his friend said, 'Old Thomas is a real old bastard isn't he?'

Whereon David remarked, 'You mean he was born out of wedlock?' and burst out laughing, even though the pain in his hands was still there. 'When Old Thomas asked me that question I was far away, I was thinking about the market so I guess I deserved the cane.'

After a few weeks David had accumulated quite a lot of timber from the cases he had taken home. Most of the local kids and a few of their fathers who kept pigeons wanted light and cheap timber, which David now had, and the nails to go with it, so he was in business and started to make money. He also used his trolley to collect sacks of coke for the old pensioners in the road. Usually when he returned with the coke he was rewarded with a small amount of money for his efforts. All of the money which he earned went into an old jam jar that he kept hidden away in his the shed.

Soon it was time for Mary to visit London and William. She was the envy of quite a few of the neighbours and her friends, and she wished that they could all go with her. Mary wore her best clothes, which she had washed and ironed especially for her visit. She carried herself well and looked very fine.

Bert kissed his wife as she got into the train and said, 'No one in London will look lovelier than you, we have a queen in London, but you are my queen,' and he meant it.

William met Mary in London, the train was on time and after giving his Ma a big kiss and an even bigger hug, he took her case in one hand and her arm in the other and so they walked down the platform and out into the London streets.

CHAPTER 4

THE STREETS WERE CROWDED with people and all kinds of transport: buses, taxis, vans and lorries. Mary had heard and read of all these things that London had, but now she was here and seeing them for herself, and could hardly believe her eyes, there seemed to be so many streets, roads and above all so many people. They travelled by the underground and then by bus, and she was fascinated by the sights and sounds that she encountered as they made their way to William's lodgings.

Eventually they reached their destination. William's rooms were in a large Victorian terrace house, which no doubt had seen better days. The landlady was introduced to Mary, who found her quite pleasant, if a little on the stiff side, 'but then perhaps that is what they are like down here in London, not like us Yorkshire folk' she thought. Mary was asked if she would like a cup of tea, which she gladly accepted and was shown up to her room.

'You are favoured Mum,' smiled William, 'mine is a back room and looks on to the yard.'

The room was very clean and tidy, there was a double bed, dressing table, wardrobe, chair and sink with hot and cold running water, and the landlady had added a vase of fresh flowers to brighten it up. William showed his Mother his bedroom and the bathroom, while the landlady went to make the tea. She soon returned with a tray on which was a pot of tea, a jug of milk, some sugar and a plate of biscuits. When Mary saw the tea tray she gave the lady a huge thank you, and a radiant smile. Once the tea was finished, Mary had a rest on her comfortable bed, as she was a little tired from the long train journey.

After a short while Mary felt refreshed, and together with William, she set out to see as many London landmarks as she could in her short stay. William took her to the places that he thought would interest her the most: they rode on the buses and also did a considerable amount of walking, so when it was time to have a meal they were both ready to sit down and rest.

William only had bed and breakfast at his lodgings, so he took Mary to one of his favourite places, The Marble Arch Corner House, which in those days was excellent value for money. The restaurant was on three separate floors; each floor had its own orchestra in national costume, which added to the ambience. The waiters were very efficient and courteous, and the food was excellent. As Mary sat there waiting to be served her thoughts went back to home, to where her neighbours and family were, for as she sat there she felt like a duchess, and she certainly did not look or feel out of place in these surroundings. She did not have to dwell too long on such thoughts as the food soon arrived: cooked just as she liked it and on nice china. Mary took time eating her meal, enjoying every morsel and making very little conversation whilst she ate. William occasionally looked at her while she was eating and noticed how much she was enjoying everything, he like the rest of the family, was so proud of her and it showed as he sat there.

'Everything satisfactory madam?' asked the waiter, when Mary had finished.

'Everything was very nice, thank you,' she answered, touching her lips with her napkin.

She had enjoyed the meal very much; in fact she had enjoyed every minute since she had arrived in London.

Whilst William was paying the bill, she retired to the powder room, and they met up again in a matter of minutes.

'Seen as though it's a pleasant evening, would you like to go for a walk, that it is if you are not too tired?' asked William.

'I'm fine,' answered Mary, 'and the walk will help digest that marvellous meal I have just had.'

She put her arm in his, and as they walked along they looked so happy, they could have been taken for a courting couple, if Mary had been a few years younger. They seemed to walk for a long time, doing a lot of talking and taking in the London nightlife and sights. They eventually got on a bus and went back to William's lodgings, where Mary was more than glad to kick off her shoes, sit down and relax before retiring for the night.

William kissed his Mum good night and retired to his room. Mary undressed, washed and put on her nightdress and got into bed. As she lay there she felt so happy; she could not remember when she had enjoyed a day like today, and she soon drifted off into a peaceful sleep.

She awoke refreshed, had a good breakfast with William and then the two of them started out on another day of sightseeing. Luck was with them and the sun shone most of the day, and so they decided to take their lunch in one of the many London parks. They shared their sandwiches with birds and sat relaxing in the lovely fresh air. When they had finished eating Mary remarked that it was a very welcome change to be free of housework and all the chores that normally filled her time, if only for a little while. In the bandstand, which was not too far away from them, a military band was playing. On hearing this she remarked, 'Aren't I lucky, I had the orchestra in the restaurant to play to me last night, and now the army has sent the band to play for me while I eat my lunch in the park.' They both laughed at this last remark, and more so when she said, 'We don't have to pay for this band, this one is free.' As they talked they sat down on a park bench, and the conversation soon turned to the subject of money, 'You're sure you can pay for meals for me?' asked Mary.

'Of course I can,' answered William. 'I wouldn't have asked you to come if I couldn't afford it. I've worked quite a lot of overtime recently, and don't you worry, thanks to your training I'm not in debt nor do I intend to be. I've saved for this visit so enjoy it, and if you are lucky we will go to the same restaurant tonight but we can sit on a different floor, with a different orchestra. I guess that after last night and today's lunch you are getting used to eating with music aren't you? Things won't be the same when you go home and you haven't got live music playing, will it?' he joked.

'Go on with you,' exclaimed Mary, 'you're spoiling me.'

'There's no one I would rather spoil, than you,' he remarked.

The time soon came for Mary's visit to London to end. William saw her safely on the train, and it was difficult who felt the saddest as they embraced before parting.

Bert met Mary at the station when she arrived home, gave her a big hug and kiss, before taking her case.

'Everything and everyone ok?' asked Mary.

'I guess so,' he replied, 'nice to see you back. Oh and our two said I'm not as good a cook as you, and I did my best, well that's gratitude for you.'

'Well I'm back now, and I'll soon be back in charge once I'm inside our home.'

The boys like Bert were pleased to see her return to them, and welcomed her back home, perhaps more in anticipation of some decent food once again. As they sat down to the first meal that Mary cooked on her return, the children pulled Bert's leg about his cooking and housekeeping, or lack of it. Mary soon got onto the topic of London and couldn't stop talking about what she had seen and where she had been, and about how good William had been to her while she was down there. She talked so much about her trip that no one else was able to say a word. When she left the room, Bert pulled a face and made a gesture as if to say that they were going to get a lot of information regarding London in the future from Mary, and they all laughed.

David continued to work at the market, and as his wood store depleted one week he replaced it the next with the empty case that he took home on his barrow. Whilst the other kids were carelessly playing in the streets, David had managed to find himself a job that was beginning to make money, which he saved in the jar in the shed.

One day when there was just him and Mary in the living room he said, 'I knew that when you went to London our William would look after you, so I kept this for when you came back as I thought it would be more useful now than when you were in London.' In his hand he held the old jam jar, which contained an assortment of coppers and small silver change that he had saved from removing the cases from the market together with the tips that he received from fetching coke from the gashouse.

'So you see my "object" as our Alfred called it, has come in useful. For without my "object" I wouldn't be able to get the wood home and make any money would I? I want you to have it, as I planned it all from the start for you, Mum.'

Mary's eyes filled with tears as she pulled him towards her and gave him a big hug.

'Thank you very much David,' she said, not wanting to hurt him or offend his feelings by refusing his hard earned gift. Here was a mere boy with the care and feeling of a man, and no age on his shoulders, wanting to help out and contribute towards the meagre housekeeping.

'Can I have the jam jar back please Mum?' he asked.

She emptied the jar, counted the coins into their respective piles, and said, 'I suppose you have counted it previously, haven't you?'

'Well yes,' he answered, 'although I have put a little bit more in the jar since I last counted it.'

With that he picked up his now empty jar, and with a cheerio was on his way. When Bert returned home she told him about what David had just done.

Bert said, 'I've seen that jar in the shed. I asked David what it was for and he said that he was "saving it up for a special person". In fact I thought he was a bit young for a girlfriend, but now I know that that girlfriend is you. I guess I should be jealous,' and with that he gave a laugh.

More rumours started going around that the docks that the shipyards would soon be reopening. This time the rumour was true as they both were to open again within two weeks. It was as if a cloud had been lifted from the whole community: no longer would groups of men be standing idle on street corners; no longer would women having to manage their homes on the dole money, even washdays seemed to be brighter days than of late. The local trades people such as the milkmen, coal men and the gas lamp lighters started to whistle and sing as they went about their daily tasks, and everyone seemed more cheerful and happy now that the town's main industry was about to be back up and running.

When Bert's family took their evening meal, naturally the main topic was of impending work, as was the case in most of the households in the neighbourhood. Unemployment had been rife for so long that people could hardly believe that once again they would have a real weekly wage coming in. Women were pleased that their men folk would be back at work and no longer in the house and under their feet, as they so aptly put it. As they collected their last lot of dole money, the men were told to report to where they had previously worked.

On their first day back when the shipyard buzzer blew at twelve noon for the men to cease work it was a marvellous sound for many people; however no one thought that in a few years time the buzzer would have a more sinister reason behind it.

Bert resumed his old job and when payday came at the weekend he couldn't cycle home quickly enough to hand Mary his first weekly wage. Bert was unlike many of his neighbours, who gave their wives only a small fraction of their earnings, and spent the rest in the local pub.

After a few weeks passed Mary was more than surprised when Alfred remarked that he was thinking of joining the Royal Air Force. As he had never mentioned it previously it came like a bolt out of the blue, and a worried look came over her face. The thought of Alfred leaving home along with William, and the break up of her family was one thing she did not relish.

'Why do you want to join up?' she asked.

'Well Dad is now back in employment and I have fancied the RAF for sometime. A couple of my pals have joined; they like it very much and are seeing the world on the cheap. The job I am doing at the present doesn't offer a lot for the future, and I think that the RAF does. You don't need my money as much now that Dad is earning again and our David will soon be at work.'

'Well you are old enough to please yourself, so whatever I say you have the final say in the matter, and I know you will please yourself,' answered Mary. 'Don't you agree Bert?'

'I don't think the planes in the RAF use trenches as we did in the war, so if I had a choice I would pick the RAF instead of the army,' said Bert.

'What kind of an answer is that?' asked Mary.

'A good and sensible one I reckon,' was his reply. 'Also the blue uniform is more attractive than the khaki one to get the girls,' he joked as he smiled and winked at Alfred.

'Just the daft sort of an answer I expected from you,' she said, as a smile came over her face.

When Alfred saw the smile on Mary's face his mind was made up and he decided that the RAF would be his life in the near future come what may.

CHAPTER 5

IN THE MONTHS THAT FOLLOWED things gradually got back to pre-strike days for the inhabitants of the old seaport. In the street where Mary lived, Granny Andrews delivered a few babies, some of the old people passed away and there were two weddings, all of which kept the cycle of life going.

Alfred had made up his mind to join the Air Force and there was no dissuading him. Mary and Bert had many discussions for and against him joining, but it was to no avail, Alfred had made up his mind. David did not enter into these discussions, he sat there listening, but never said a word, in case he was told to mind his own business, as no doubt he would have been. The thought of having a brother in the Air Force rather thrilled him, no doubt he thought that all Air Force personnel were pilots and all had a plane to fly.

William paid the odd visit home when he could manage the time off from work; he had been promoted and had had a substantial rise in salary that pleased his parents. So far he had not brought a lady friend to visit, but by the conversation both Bert and Mary surmised that he was seeing someone back in London. Alfred had a few girlfriends, all local girls, but nothing serious, so he would leave no broken hearts when the time came for him to leave home. The day finally came, and just as she had waved goodbye to William, she waved goodbye to her middle son as he started out on his new life in the Air Force.

With Alfred now in the Air Force the house seemed strange to Mary, the family was now down to just the three of them. There was less food to prepare and less washing and ironing to do, but she missed the work that her absent sons produced. For so many years she had had a large family to bring up and she was loathe to accept the change. Her life had changed so much in such a short time since the two boys had left home.

Her three boys were all different in temperament and in their outlook on life. William was careful to a point and Alfred was more suited to life in the services than his older brother would have been. Then there was David; quiet, tall, always thinking ahead, helpful, tidy in most of his ways and very careful, almost too careful, where money was concerned. Three people all belonging to her and Bert, but all so different, and she was so proud of her "brood" as she called them when referring to them.

Alfred wrote home, but not as often as William had when he left home, but Mary had not expected him to. William's letters were not as frequent nowadays, but she was always pleased to receive one, even if it was short, and he had a lady friend now and said that he hoped that he could introduce her to them, and that they would approve of his choice. Bert and Mary longed to meet her and were sure that they would like her. From his letters, they could tell that Alfred had settled down in his new life in the Air Force, even though the discipline was very strict. He was to learn a new trade and when fully trained he would be posted anywhere in the world.

Christmas was not many weeks away, the weather had changed and winter was on its way. Attractive goods were on display in the illuminated shop windows; this Christmas they appeared more attractive as people had more money to spend than in the past few years. William wrote saying that he would be home for the festive few days, but would be coming alone, much to the disappointment of Mary and Bert, who were still longing to meet the girlfriend. Alfred said that he would be on leave for at least seven days at Christmas and that he would be home. Knowing that her family would all be together for a few days, and sensing that this might be the last Christmas that they were all together, Mary was very busy preparing cakes and puddings and pies as well as buying presents. She so much wanted to make this Christmas a special and memorable one.

David continued to work at the market when he could, and it was surprising how many of the market people came to rely on his services and to give him payment, which he gladly took. He also had some money in his pocket so he could give change if required so that no one owed him or forgot to pay him. David soon became known in the town as "that lad with the cart", who always seemed to be working at something and earning in one way or the other.

David was nearly ready for leaving his school days behind him, his teachers said he was average at his lessons, and that if he would pay attention he could be in the top stream, but usually he was not attentive enough, and his mind was on other things. He may not have focussed all his energy on his schoolwork, but he had taught himself in matters of business, and he felt that this was to be the most valuable education he could have.

One day when David was walking home from school he saw the figure of a teenage girl further up the road. She had her back up to the wall; in her arms she was holding a violin case, which she held tight. Standing in front of her was a large cur of a crossbred dog, its teeth were bared and it was snarling and looked as though it was ready to attack at any moment. As he got nearer to the girl he could see how frightened and petrified she looked. None of the passers by seemed to take any notice of the poor girl's plight; looking around he noticed a galvanised dustbin with a very heavy lid. Taking off the lid he rolled it on its side with all his force catching the brute of a beast in the mid ribs, knocking the breath from its body. As the lid hit the dog, David ran towards it shouting with his arms outstretched. The dog by now had partially recovered from the blow of the dustbin lid, dropped its tail between its legs and quickly ran off down the road. Looking up at the girl he smiled. 'Oh thank you, thank you,' she said, 'I was so scared.'

'I could see that. It's lucky we had this so near,' he said as he replaced the dustbin lid. 'Come on, I know where you live and I'm going your way so we can walk together.'

David had seen this girl quite a few times previously but had not taken any interest in her, or in any other girl yet in his life, girls were not of interest to him. As they walked along the colour gradually returned to her cheeks, for when David first saw her she was as white as a ghost, but she soon felt more at ease, as she talked to David, who she saw as her knight in shining armour, even if he wasn't on horseback. They soon reached the pawnshop where she lived, once again she thanked him and they said goodbye. Once inside the house, Rosa as she was called, could not tell her mother and father quick enough what had happened to her with the dog, and how David was the only one to help her, and how he had brought her home safe.

'Who is this boy Rosa? Do I know him? Does he come to our shop?' asked her father.

'No I've never seen him in the shop Daddy,' replied Rosa, ' but I did recognise him. Maybe you have seen him pushing a funny handcart with bits of wood on it. He always appears very clean and tidy and I once heard someone call him David. But today I did not ask him his name, nor did he ask mine, we just walked and talked.

'If the boy's name is David, then I like it, for it's a good Jewish name, but I don't suppose he is Jewish, or has Jewish parents, do you?' replied her father. 'Still I would like to meet this boy and thank him personally for helping my Rosa in her hour of great need, maybe one day we will meet him.'

When David arrived home he did not mention the episode regarding the girl and the dog to his family. They would never have known, unless someone had not told Bert that they had seen David walking a girl home and that she was Jewish.

Bert mentioned what he had learnt one evening during teatime. David explained to Mary and Bert what had happened, and they were very proud of him for helping the girl, and said that they hoped no one would think that he was being cruel to the dog if they had not seen the whole incident.

'I don't care,' answered David, 'I just felt that I had to help the girl and I did.'

'Fair enough,' said Bert, 'we were only teasing you about

having a girlfriend. But now your school days are nearly over and you are soon to start work fulltime, you are growing up and I guess no doubt sooner or later a girl will play a part in your life. I only hope your choice will be as happy as your mother and I have been throughout the years.'

A week or so later David was at the station waiting for the train to arrive with a consignment of rabbits that he was to take back to the market on his barrow. Now that the weather was colder, rabbits were in demand, as rabbit meat was still a cheap meal, and the public had now acquired a taste for them.

Rosa's Father, Mr Levine, or Uncle Ike as he was known locally, was about to meet David sooner than he had anticipated. He too was expecting a packing case to be delivered by train so had gone to the railway station to enquire of its whereabouts and was more than pleased to see David with his barrow there. He hoped that David would deliver it to the shop if and when it arrived.

Walking up to the lad Mr Levine said, 'I believe you are David, am I correct?'

'Yes sir, that is my name. Can I be of any help?' David replied.

'I hope so,' said Mr Levine, and he explained about the expected case, and then enquired about how much David charged for his service.

'That depends on the size of the object and the distance of the delivery,' answered David.

Mr Levine could hardly believe his ears, this answer curt, polite and as quick as could be and from a mere boy amazed him, and even more so when David said, 'I think you'll find my rates very competitive.'

David continued, 'Sir if your case is on this train I must deliver the goods that I have come down here for first, and then I will deliver your goods to your given destination as promptly as I can.'

Thanking each other they moved apart and walked down the platform. David took delivery of his rabbits from the guard's van, went to the office and signed for them and went on his way. Mr Levine's packing case was on the same train; David saw Mr Levine and the porter pushing it along the platform so he knew it had arrived, and he would come back for it later.

As Mr Levine walked back to his home and shop he could not get this young lad out of his head. When Rosa had told him of the way David had saved her from the dog he had been somewhat surprised at the way he had acted so swiftly and efficiently in the situation, but having now met him he realised that it had been true.

Meanwhile David had delivered his load of fresh rabbits, and enquired if he would be needed for an hour or so, when told no he wouldn't, he proceeded to the station, picked up the case and soon delivered it to the Levines' shop.

When Mr Levine saw him and the packing case he remarked, 'My that's quick service my lad, are you always so prompt?'

'I try to be sir,' was his reply. 'Where would you like it putting?' He had grown into a big strong lad now and picked up the case with ease.

'Over there will you?' said Mr Levine pointing to a space on the shop floor. 'How much do I owe you?'

'It was not a huge case and not too far a distance to deliver to, so if you are agreeable to the middle rate I quoted sir, I will be well satisfied and hope you will be to,' said David.

'I am well satisfied my lad. Up until I saw you at the station I was wondering how I was going to get it home, it would not do my image any good for my customers to see an old man pushing a barrow with a case on top, would it?' and gave a laugh as he said it. Before he paid David he said, 'I have never thanked you for saving Rosa from that dog. Mrs Levine is out just now and I know that she wants to thank you also, so if you can come around in the near future for a visit, we can both show our appreciation to you, and I know Rosa will be pleased to see you also.'

They said their goodbyes and David proceeded to go about his business. The weather changed and it looked as if the folk would be in for a white Christmas. William and Alfred arrived and quickly settled into their old home. William looked very handsome in a new suit, as did Alfred in his RAF uniform and both looked a credit to Mary and Bert's upbringing.

This year there were more presents given to one another than in the past few years, and the Christmas fare was a joy to behold. The praise shown to Mary was enough to make her head swell. Unfortunately the festive days were soon over and it was back to work as usual, and once again Mary was back to a small family, as her two elder sons returned to their new homes.

David finished school and had a few days holiday before he started a full time job down at the shipyard. The docks rarely employed school leavers, preferring to use more experienced older men, but Bert had managed to help David get a job. David didn't fancy shipyard work and made it known to both Mary and Bert, but with no alternative direction for him to take he reluctantly agreed to give the shipyard a try. He was soon taken on and being a big, strong youth he could stand his corner with the men of the yard, however he still remained quiet and somewhat reserved, and was still the thinker. Whatever job he was put to he did quickly, and wherever he went in the shipyard he never missed a trick taking notice and remembering how things were done. In fact there was not much that David did not notice in everyday life. He had noticed that most of the men, like his father, used a bicycle to get to and from work, and he saw this as a potential business opportunity.

Even though he was now working from half past seven in the morning to five 'o'clock, he still continued to go to the market as he had always done. The mode of packaging changed, wood was now being replaced by cardboard, so there was less need for him at the market nowadays and this meant less money. Also now that the men were back in work at the shipyards they did not now require David's timber from the packing cases.

As David walked home from work one day, he noticed an old cycle had been discarded on a rubbish tip, walking over he noticed that the frame was in good condition and although the handlebars were bent, he knew that they would straighten out. He pulled the bike from the tip, but it would not wheel so picking it up he placed it over his shoulder and proceeded to walk home.

David's young moneymaking mind started to work, and a few days later he asked his father if he was ever thinking of keeping pigs again.

'I doubt it very much. Betsy served us very well when we needed her most and we had many a good meal we would not have had, but there's only three of us and we have a little more brass and I guess we can afford to buy our pork and bacon from the butcher now. Anyway why do you ask? You're not thinking of keeping pigs are you?'

'No Dad, but now the sty isn't in use I was wondering if you and I could convert it into a shed, only a small one. I have enough wood to replace and mend the sides.'

'I don't see why not. But what do you want a shed for?'

'To build my bike up,' was the answer.

'Yes, I saw you had found an old frame from somewhere, and I hoped it wasn't going to stay in the yard for long, or you or me would soon be feeling your mother's tongue. There won't be much light to work inside that shed though.'

'I've thought of that,' said David 'and I hope I can get a fairly good window soon. As I was walking from work the other day, I bumped into Les Garner who said his mother was going to have a new larger window put in her kitchen. Mr Garner has won some money on the pools, and his Mum's share of the winnings is going on the window. Anyway I asked if I could have the old window and would she ask the workmen to be careful with the glass when they removed it. Les asked her and she said yes, so Dad, I've already sorted that.'

'Ok, when they take out the window we'll make a start on the shed,' said Bert. 'One of my joiner pals owes me a favour and will help us, no doubt he'll make a more professional job of it than us. That cart of yours will come in useful when we go to deliver the window from Mrs Garner's.'

Bert loved and admired all his family, but somehow his feelings for David were different, a stronger bond had grown between them than he felt for either William or Alfred, and it was a feeling that he could not describe to anyone, not even Mary. Maybe it was because he was the youngest; indeed David was far different in attitude to the two older boys.

Within a few weeks Mrs Garner's window was put in place, she was very pleased with it as it did let in more light. As asked she instructed the workmen to be careful removing the old frame and glass, and they obeyed her instructions. As promised David came along with his cart and was able to take it away, much to her delight.

CHAPTER 6

THE SUN CAME, the weather improved and summer arrived. David's shed was now complete and no longer resembled Betsy's old sty. Bert's friend, the joiner, had certainly made a good job of rebuilding it, and David had given the boards a coat of creosote and the window a lick of paint so that it was now the most impressive shed on the allotment.

Now that the shed was completed, David was ready to start to reconstruct the bicycle. First he removed everything down to the frame, discarding anything that was unserviceable, and making sure that he knew where each and every part had come from, so that when he came to reassemble the cycle everything went back into its correct position. After nearly wearing out the wire brush and many sheets of emery paper he managed to get the frame more or less down to base metal. He had saved enough money to buy enamel paint for the frame, and gave the bike several coats until it shone like a new penny. The handlebars straightened out with a little help from a blowlamp, which he gently applied so as not to damage the chrome or discolour it. He added new wheel rims, spokes, pedals, chain, sprockets and saddle. The purchasing of all these items soon depleted most of his savings, but at least he had a bicycle now.

David kept his new project of bike repairing to himself and didn't even tell Mary who kept enquiring about why he was spending all his free time in the shed at the allotment. Bert didn't interfere, and when he was at the allotment deliberately kept out of David's way. When he had completed the bike, David took it for a ride before taking it to show his Mum and Dad. When Mary and Bert saw what a fine job he had made of it they were filled with pride and emotion, and it showed.

When David told the men and lads at work that he had repaired his cycle himself, they were amazed at the job he had done, as most of them thought it was a new one. Within a short period of time word spread around the yard, and he was soon asked if he would do repairs on their bikes when they were needed. David's plan had worked: his new bike was acting as a good advertisement for his business, and his hard work was starting to pay off. He hoped that this new undertaking would be even more successful than his cart business, and it definitely would be easier on his limbs, as pushing the cart around had been hard work.

One night after work, towards the end of the summer, David was cycling home when he bumped into Rosa. Both noted how the other had changed and grown up since their last meeting. Rosa was taller and slimmer, her hair was darker and longer and her smile, which lit up her face on seeing David again, gave her an aura that he had never seen before. To her, David had changed, here now was a young man, strong, tall and looking as clean as he always did, even though his work at the shipyard was dirty. He may have grown bigger and looked older but she knew that his temperament and personality had not changed, nor did she think it ever would. After a hurried conversation about how David had met Rosa's father at the station and done a small job for him, and how he would like to meet her mother, they parted and waved goodbye to each other.

When David arrived home he told Mary how he had seen and met Rosa again, and how she had changed and now looked so grown up. He didn't say how lovely she looked, he was too diplomatic for that, but she could read between the lines and understood what he meant. Later that night when they were alone, Mary told Bert how David had met Rosa again in town, and how she thought Rosa had made an impression on him.

'Well my love, if she has impressed him on their second meeting like you impressed me on our second meeting, I guess he has had it,' answered Bert.

'That is what I'm afraid of. They're both so young, and I don't want either of them to get hurt. Don't forget she's

Jewish and could never marry our David. If it ever came to it they would have to decide how much they loved each, other and it could cause so much pain to both of them. It's because of that I hope that they never do fall in love with each other. Don't say a word to our David about what we have been discussing Bert, and lets hope we're wrong in what we're thinking, and that things do work out for the best in the end. Now would you like a cup of tea Bert?' and with this their conversation came to an end as she got up from her chair to put the kettle on.

When Rosa returned home she, like David, told her parents how she had met up with him again, and how he had grown in stature and seemed very adult for his years. As she told her Mama and Papa her face lit up and she looked so happy.

'I asked him to visit us, so he could meet you Mama as I know you have never met him,' said Rosa.

'Get your meal my dear,' said her Mother, 'and we will talk about things together later, Papa has something he wants to say to you, ok.'

Later that night when they were sitting down in the lounge her father gave a little cough, more to draw attention than to clear his throat, and said, 'You know my Rosa,' as "my Rosa" was his favourite way of addressing her, 'you know your Mama and I love you very much, and there is nothing we would not do for you or give you if it were possible. When we left Russia we had to leave many of our possessions behind, but one thing we did not leave behind was our faith and our religion, we are Jewish as you are aware.'

'Of course I am,' came the reply.

'The boy David, we know you like him, and what I have seen of him I can't see how you couldn't like him, but please don't get too involved, you are both young, and you know that nothing could come from this friendship. A Jew and a gentile can never marry and raise a family, it's wrong in every way.'

Rosa let her Father finish, and then said with a smile, 'David and I have only met twice, and I don't suppose he's interested in me, maybe he has a girlfriend already. Anyway, I'm going to France in the near future to study music, so we couldn't meet, even if we wanted to. Who knows Papa, maybe you'll end up with a dark haired, real Jewish boy as a son-in-law. You don't have to worry just yet, anyway, because my music comes first,' and with that she gave a huge laugh and departed saying, 'I'm going to wash my hair now, see you in a little while.'

Mr and Mrs Levine looked at each other when she left the room, and both knew what the other was thinking. Rosa would not let her feelings, if she was interested in David, get too deep, as she would not allow herself to end up being hurt. Both hoped for the sake of their daughter that David did have other girl friends, and that Rosa wasn't one of them.

Everyday David joined the sea of cyclists that rode to and from work twice a day. It was not surprising that most of the men didn't take as good care of their bikes as David took of his, and so they often needed to be repaired. This meant that David's services were forever in demand, and when he was not at the shipyard he could be found in his shed. He had purchased a medium sized Tilley lamp, which gave adequate illumination in the small shed to work by when the light was failing. The small shed didn't have a huge amount of workspace, but every inch was put to good use: he had put up some shelves, on which were many boxes labelled nuts and bolts – everything had a home. He kept any damaged part of a cycle that could be used later, and those that were beyond repair he soon discarded, so as not to cause the slightest amount of rubbish and clutter. He seemed to relish the work he was doing, and spent many hours on his own working away. He found that the more jobs he did the more he enjoyed it and the better he got. As his charges were not as high as any of the cycle repairs in town, he was often asked to do a lot of work, but he was careful to just take on as much work as he could manage, as he did not want any aggravation or unpleasantness if the job was not completed on time.

Working at the shipyard had never really appealed to him, and because of his job he found that he had to turn down a lot of cycle repair work. The standard of his workmanship was very good compared to repairers in the town, and if he said a price and time of completion he kept to his word, which meant a lot to his customers.

One day at lunchtime he had gone into town shopping, when he noticed a shop that had been empty for some considerable time. Dismounting from his cycle, which he propped up at the curb's edge, he went to the shop window and looked inside. The shop had a good floor space and appeared to be dry, in one corner he could see that it contained a toilet and sink, and that was all.

Later that day when the family were taking tea, David said, 'Dad, have you ever thought of renting a shop?'

'What, me rent a shop, whatever for?'

'Me,' David said. 'There is one on the High Street that has been empty for a long time. I guess you could get it cheap, as the owners would no doubt rent it out to you, but I guess they would not let it to me, no doubt they would say I was too young. You know how busy I have been at the shed doing my cycle repairs, well there's no longer enough room, and above all not enough time. You know that the job at the yard is not really for me, and that I have never really liked it. Just imagine if I had all day to do my repairs, think how many I could do in a week. I would work really hard at it.'

'I know you'd work hard. Your Mother and I say you work too many hours now, but we don't wish to interfere. We'll talk it over and let you have a decision soon, but don't be too disappointed if we say no son.'

After the meal finished David soon disappeared to his shed and wouldn't be back until bedtime. Now that they were alone, Bert said, 'Come on Mary let's go for a walk and take a look at this shop, then later we can talk things over.'

They didn't often go for a walk on an evening, so it made

a welcome change which both of them enjoyed. Bert took Mary's arm in his, and both agreed it reminded them of their courting days, as they strolled towards the High Street. They knew where the shop was situated so first viewed it from the opposite side of the road before crossing over the street to look through the empty window. The shop was in a row of shops with flats above, all of which appeared to have tenants in occupation. There was no cycle shop anywhere near the area and both agreed that David had made a good choice for his cycle shop, should it come about. Mary tested the window frame and door, by poking and prodding them with her fingers, and they all seemed to pass her inspection. As they could not go inside and take a look at the interior, they decided to make their way home.

They had not walked far when Bert said, 'You know Mary, I think if anyone could make a go of that bike shop business, our David could. What the lad lacks in years he makes up for in common sense, don't you agree?'

'I was hoping you would say that, since seeing its position I think it could be the ideal spot. Tomorrow whilst you are at work, I'll contact the agents, and find out about the rent and if there is a lease. I hope there is not a lease, as one could take some getting rid of if the business failed. The front could do with a lick of paint, so if the owners would waive the first month's rent, and we painted it that at least would help our David make a start. Nothing ventured nothing gained, at least it's worth a try, and people are not queuing to rent the shop are they? Not a word to anyone about what we are about to do, and least of all to our David until things are finalised, do you hear Bert, keep you mouth shut for once.'

'Now I know where he gets his ideas and business head from. I didn't think he got it from me,' replied Bert. 'It's attributes like that, that make me love you so,' and with that he took her in his arms and gave her a little squeeze as they walked on.

Next morning true to her word, Mary went to the agent

who was in charge of letting the shop. Luckily she knew the man, and he was most helpful in every way. There was no lease on letting so that was in her favour, but as for the month's free rent, the agent didn't give a lot of hope, but said that he would do his best for them. The agent would discuss their proposals with the owner of the shop and report back to Mary and Bert with the outcome as soon as possible.

David and Bert always came home for lunch together, so it was after tea, when David had gone to the shed, before Mary and Bert were alone and able to discuss the details of her visit to the estate agent.

'If we do manage to rent the shop, and that they accept our offer to paint it as the first month's payment, then David will be able to earn enough to buy furniture and decorate the interior. He could also buy some posters and put them up in the window. This with the new paintwork will help make it look more businesslike.'

'One thing I want to know,' asked Bert, 'who's going to get the job of painting the shop, me?'

'Of course,' answered Mary, 'who else?'

Eventually they received a letter asking them to call at the agents, so that they could make things formal, as they were to be the new tenants of the shop. The letter also stated that the owner had agreed to their proposal to paint the outside of the shop instead of the first month's rent. It was not until later, when David had eaten his tea, that Mary gave him the letter to read. His face lit up, and he was excited at the prospect of his new business growing.

'I never expected this to happen; it's like a dream come true Mum. Aren't I lucky in having such wonderful parents? I don't like working at the shipyard, I was prepared to stay there, but now this has happened I can do something I really like doing, and also try and make some money for us all, and even if it's not huge amounts it'll help.'

On the agreed day the keys to the shop were handed over, and at the weekend all three were there helping to prepare for the opening. Bert scraped the paint from the windowpane, not daring to use a blowtorch in case he cracked the glass, and then sanded down the frames until the wood was as smooth as silk. He painted a couple of undercoats, and later added a final coat of high gloss paint; even Bert thought what a good job he had made of it, which indeed he had. Once they had finished all the painting, cleaning, sweeping and washing, the shop had been transformed from the empty shell of a building to a potentially prosperous business, and all this had been achieved through a lot of hard work, but very little expense.

When David went back to work on Monday, he gave in his notice. As the work force turnover was high at the shipyard no one took any interest in why he was leaving. He worked his final week, and as usual did as many repairs at the shed as he could, and began to make preparations for his move from the shed to the new shop at the weekend. There were quite a few cycles to be moved to the shop to be repaired, so once again his cart would come in very useful.

When Saturday came, he made several trips between the shed and the new shop. His cart was loaded with bicycles and spare parts and many people thought his new business was as a rag and bone man.

Newly printed posters advertising his business were placed at angles in the shop window, along with a notice saying that he was open for business. Mary had bought him a long, grey coat to wear inside the shop whilst he was doing his repairs, so that in every aspect he presented a professional image. With no other cycle repair shop in that area of town it was not long before he had enquiries coming, which seemed an encouraging start. After only being able to work evenings and weekends, it was surprising how many repairs he was able to do in a full day. He worked hard at his business, to make it a success, and surprised himself at the amount of work he could achieve now that he had more time.

CHAPTER 7

TIME SEEMED TO FLY so fast, and weeks soon turned into months and Mary and Bert were more than pleased to see that the venture had taken off successfully. Both helped David whenever they could: Mary with bookings and the ordering of material, and Bert as a general labourer. Between them they all worked very well together, and their efforts were much appreciated.

One day when the shop door opened, who should be standing there but Rosa. 'Hello, how are you? Someone told me this shop had been reopened but I didn't know by whom. I looked through the window as I was passing by and of course recognised you. How are you?'

'Very well, thank you, and you?' he answered.

The conversation continued and she eventually told him that she would soon be off to Paris to live and study music. She also reminded him that he had never met her mother, and so asked him if he would like to visit them this Sunday and take afternoon tea with them. A customer came into the shop and their discussion came to an end, but he agreed to take up her invitation and visit them on Sunday.

When David arrived home he told his mum and dad of his intentions for the coming Sunday. They were happy to let him go, but both breathed a sigh of relief when he said that she was going to live in Paris, and would be away indefinitely. They both agreed that it was nice for him to have met her again and hoped that they would have a pleasant meeting on Sunday.

Rosa arrived home and explained how she had met up with David again, and had accepted her invitation to visit them on Sunday. 'I hope that will be OK?' she asked.

'Of course it will,' answered her mother, 'the fact that I'm about to meet him at last really pleases me, and if your Papa likes him, then I am sure I will too.'

Sunday arrived and what a lovely day it was: warm and

sunny, but not too hot. David looked so smart and handsome and was soon ready to go and meet the Levine family in their home. With it being such a nice day he did not hurry as he walked along, and really enjoyed the walk to their home. After being so busy the previous weekends, it was really enjoyable to relax and take in the beauty of the flowers in window boxes and small gardens, and even the sky seemed to have taken on a brighter shade of blue.

In the past, as a child at school, David had been told that the Levines were Jewish, and that they were different to the rest of us. It was easy then to become prejudiced, but as he grew older David soon dismissed this intolerance, and was looking forward to meeting the Levines as a family. Their home although situated above the shop had a separate side entrance, and he had to wait a moment or two to be let in. Although he had passed by the shop many times in the past, he had never taken particular notice of it, even though he knew that Rosa lived there. Everything looked so clean, neat and tidy, even the bell pull shone like glass, and one could see that it had a daily polish, which indeed it had over many years. Rosa opened the door and gave him a huge smile; she looked magnificent standing there before him, she was wearing a bright red dress which fitted like a glove, her black shoes shone and her dark almost black hair fell over her shoulders to make a perfect picture and one that would stay in David's mind for a long time to come.

'Do please come in,' she said, 'marvellous day isn't it?' David entered, and she led him in to meet her parents who were in the lounge.

'This is my Mama, you and Papa have already met haven't you?' she said.

'So nice to meet you Mrs Levine,' said David, and shook her hand as she rose from her chair. As their eyes met for the first time, David could see where Rosa had inherited her good looks. Although not identical it was easy to see that they were related, and Mrs Levine carried her age very well.

'I am so pleased to make your acquaintance,' replied Rosa's mother, 'as I have heard so much about you from Mr Levine and Rosa.'

'All good I hope?' answered David, with a wry smile.

'Well so far,' was her answer, and she too gave a smile.

Mrs Levine provided an excellent tea for them and David did not feel uncomfortable in their company in any way, even when Mr Levine gave thanks for the food in Yiddish. All four of them seemed so comfortable and at ease together, and each of them enjoyed the afternoon and the company very much. During the conversation when David recalled the incident with the dog, he remarked how Rosa had held her violin case so close to her and that she would not even let him carry the case as they walked home. It was then that Mr Levine said that the case contained a violin of great age that had been in the Levine family for many years, and that they had brought it with them when they left Russia. He said that he wasn't musical in any way, and although he loved music he could not play himself, unlike his grandfather, who used to play the same violin years ago and whose talent had now appeared in Rosa. It was because of this that she was going to Paris to study music in the near future.

Turning to David he asked, 'Are you musical?'

'I wish I was,' answered David, 'but alas I'm not.'

'Before David leaves please play him a piece of music you think he will like Rosa,' her father instructed.

She arose from where she was sitting and went over to where she kept her violin. Placing a clean piece of cloth on her shoulder she tuned up the instrument, and then began to play. Emotionally she invested everything she possessed as she played, and she admitted to her parents later that evening that she thought that she had never played a piece of music so well before. David sat as if hypnotised by her playing.

'What is the name of that piece of music?' he asked when she had finished.

'"Fascination",' she replied, 'do you like it?'

'Like it, I think it's wonderful,' little realising what an impact that tune would have on his life from that day on.

'Before you go David, Mrs Levine and I have a little gift for you, well I have, and Mama has one for Rosa,' and with this he took from his coat pocket a small silver medallion that he gave to David. At the same time Mama put her hand into the neck of her dress and pulled out an identical one that she gave to Rosa.

'These two St Christopher medallions travelled with us from our homeland many years ago, and we have never been without them since they were given to us as we started out on our journey. They have kept us safe for many years, and now we want you to have one each, and hope that they will keep you safe wherever your life's journey takes you in the future.'

Rosa took the one from her mother and put it round her neck, the fine chain was of a good quality and the medallion expertly crafted. Rosa kissed her mother and gave her a huge hug.

'If you don't mind sir, I'll carry my medallion in my pocket for now and put it around my neck when I undress,' said David as he shook Mr Levine by the hand and thanked him very much.

'You are now in business I hear,' remarked the old man, 'I wish you every success for now and the future.' Then he said three things that David did not take a great deal of notice, but in the future would remember and reflect on the old man's wisdom. Mr Levine said, '"One swallow never makes a summer", "from a small acorn a giant oak may grow" and "never try to hold a rainbow".'

The last of his sayings seemed to have more emphasise in a strange sort of way, for as he said it he first looked at David then Rosa and finally to his wife, in a way that David could hardly comprehend, but somehow had a strange sort of meaning just for a moment. This was over as quick as it was said, and their conversation soon returned to normal.

The time soon came for them to say goodbye, and Rosa showed David to the door. Now that they were alone the old man said to his wife, 'What do you think to this David then Mother?'

'I think he is fine, and if I was much younger I'm sure that I would be tempted to fall in love with him, in fact I'm not sure I haven't done so already,' she said with a huge laugh and a saucy look towards her husband. 'I'm not passed it yet you know, although you may think I am.'

Rosa and David stood at the open door looking at each other, David asking one or two more questions: when she was leaving for Paris, what day, what time, what train? Neither dared suggest that they keep in touch. Finally he took her hand, held it tight as he shook it and said, 'Good luck in your new life. I wish you well in every way and please take good care of yourself.'

He let her hand go, and walked away. He turned around before she closed the door, stepped back and kissed her once on the cheek, and then hurried away. When Rosa returned to the room she smiled at her parents and thanked them for being so welcoming to David, and with that she went to her bedroom with a slight tear in her eye.

Trade in the shop did not slow down in the weeks to come, if anything it seemed to increase. One or two of the customers enquired whether David had thought about stocking new bicycles, as the fashion at present was for the new racing kind with the low handlebars. So when the representative called for the order of new parts, David asked him about selling bikes. The representative was only too pleased to give David all the information he could with a view to more business coming his way in the future. The profit margin on new bicycles was fairly good, and if they were bought on hire purchase the company took the risk. After quite a lot of consultation with Mary and Bert, David decided that they should give it a try. When the delivery of the new stock arrived David displayed them in the shop window and it certainly did make a huge difference as the shop was now selling as well as repairing bicycles, and it was surprising how many people were interested in purchasing a new one.

The day soon came for Rosa to leave home and to take up her studies in France. Her parents accompanied her to the station to see her make a safe start on her journey and the beginning of her musical career. David had remembered the time of her train departure from their last meeting, and was also at the station to see her depart. He kept out of view of Rosa and her family, as he knew it was a difficult thing for them to part and did not wish to intervene on their private farewell. Even though they all appeared to be so happy, he knew it was an emotional time for each of them, and didn't wish to intrude even though he wanted to be there to kiss and hug her goodbye. He, too, waited until the train left the platform, and waved goodbye from behind a window where he knew that Rosa wouldn't see him.

Alfred had more or less completed his training and was awaiting a posting overseas. William who had settled and made his home and life in London was very busy, or so he said in his letters. They were still as frequent now as they had always been and kept the family informed about his lady friend.

One day David suggested that Mary and Bert should pay a visit to London for a weekend to visit William, so that they could be introduced to this elusive girlfriend of his, otherwise they may have a new daughter-in-law who they had never met. After quite a bit of discussion, Mary and Bert agreed to visit William at his convenience, and it was soon arranged. David convinced them that he didn't need anyone to care for him whilst they were away, and that he was a big boy now and could look after himself, which he said with a huge grin.

Mary and Bert had their few days away, and really enjoyed their short visit to London. Bert thought London had changed since he was last there during the Great War, and in those days everything looked different. When they returned home it showed on their faces how much they had enjoyed themselves while they had been in London. Mary and Bert had been introduced to William's girlfriend and were favourably impressed with her, although Mary had said that she didn't think that she could make Yorkshire pudding, but she would teach her when she paid a visit to Yorkshire.

One day a young lady came into David's shop and left her cycle to be repaired. She asked if David could do her a favour in delivering it to where she would be working that evening, which was at the other end of town and it would be late when she finished work. If he delivered it to the back of the house where she was working, she would pay him plus any delivery charge. The house was the Manor House, where a ball was being held that evening, and David's new customer was to help out. He agreed to what she had requested, repaired her cycle and took it home with him and later that evening delivered it to the Manor House at the agreed time. He had a leisurely ride there, as it was a pleasant summer's evening.

The lady was there as she had promised, and she paid David for the repair and was pleased when there wasn't any delivery charge, and thanked him very much. As David walked from the rear of the house to the side of the building he had to pass the ballroom where the dance was in progress. He was half in the shadows and was not conspicuous to any of those inside. As he stood there the present dance ended, the music and tempo changed as the orchestra started up with the tune "Fascination". The orchestra was playing it well, but as he stood there he thought how much better it would have sounded if Rosa was playing with them. To him it was a marvellous piece of music and always would be.

As the tune came to an end, he started to walk down the driveway remembering how lovely Rosa had looked in her red dress that night as she had played that tune to him. He began to think about her and hoped that she had found happiness in her new life in Paris. He had not walked far when he stopped and retraced his steps back to where he had been standing listening to the music and watching the dancers. He stood in the shadows as before and thought, what a lovely sight they made: the men in their dress suits and the ladies looking so elegant in their long evening gowns. Everyone looked so happy and was smiling as they kept in step with the orchestra. At the end of the drive he stopped, did a half turn looking back to the large Manor House and thought, 'One of these days I will own a house like this, if not grander, and I will hold a ball and dance like those dancers even though I can't dance a step now.'

The evening was a marvellous one for walking and he enjoyed the journey home, which he reached somewhat quicker than he had hoped for. At home, as was usual at this time of the evening Mary was sat sewing. 'Hello son, enjoyed your walk home?' she said. 'I'll get you a drink and a bite to eat in a minute.'

'No hurry Mum,' he replied, 'I can wait for a while.' He took his jacket off and washed his hands in the kitchen sink and then returned to the room where they sat. 'Mum, can you dance the ballroom style? You and Dad never go dancing, so I was wondering if either of you can dance?'

A broad smile came over Mary's face as she stood up from her chair. 'Whatever makes you ask that?' she enquired. 'Of course your Dad and I can dance, that's how I first met him, at a dance, many years ago before the war; we were young and carefree in those days. I remember how he came over to where I was sitting and asked me if I'd care to have the next dance. He looked so handsome, and I was thrilled to think he chose me over the many other girls that he could have asked. That dance was the start of our romance, and the rest you know.'

'When I took the cycle to the Manor House there was a dance in progress and I stayed and watched the dancers pass the ballroom windows. As I cannot dance I thought that maybe you could teach me a few basic steps.'

She laughed to herself as she left the room, and thought, 'Thank you David for bringing a little reminder back into my life of those far off days, when Bert and I danced the night away at the local dance hall.' When she told Bert later of David's request they both had a laugh and remarked that David was a man in more ways than one now.

In the next week Mary bought a new record for their old gramophone, and could hardly wait until the evening when she would begin teaching David the steps. It was many years since she had danced and it would bring memories of her youth back to her. They were to have the lessons in the small parlour, and so had to push the furniture to the sides of the room to create a dance floor. The gramophone was wound up and the record placed on the turntable and they made a start. At first David had two left feet, but as the night wore on the better he became. As he held Mary in his arms she thought how firm he held her and yet how gentle and protective he seemed to be, and with more practice what an ideal partner he would make. When the time came to stop for the night both David and Mary agreed how much they had enjoyed the lesson, and laughed when they said how many times they had had to stop to rewind the gramophone and change sides on the record.

When David was taking his evening meal one night, Mary remarked that she had seen a poster for a dance which was going to be held in the town hall that coming weekend, and she thought that David should attend to see how he would shape up on a large dance floor with live music and different partners.

'I'll go on one condition,' David replied, 'and that is if you and Dad will come also, a pupil always has to perform before his teacher, and as you were my teacher I guess you cannot decline my request, now can you?' Bending over, as he rose from the table he gave Mary a kiss on her cheek.

'Oh alright,' said Mary, 'just this once, and I know your

Dad'll enjoy it after so many years away from a dance floor.'

CHAPTER 8

THE WEEKEND CAME and a taxi arrived to take them to the dance. David, Bert and Mary were all looking forward to their evening out together. David and Bert wore their best lounge suits, and Mary her new dress, which she had bought especially for the event. They all looked so smart, and David was very proud of them, and they him.

There was an excellent dance floor, and Mary and Bert soon took to it - it was as if they had danced every week since they first met. David stood back and watched them for a couple of dances and then told Bert that he was going to share the next dance with his mum. When the band started to play David politely asked Mary, 'Can I have this dance?'

'It would be a pleasure, son,' she replied. David had been an excellent pupil and they looked so natural dancing together. When the dance came to a close Mary said, 'Now, you go and find a much younger partner than me to dance with, or your Dad'll be jealous if you dance too many with me.' She gave David a huge smile and kissed his cheek.

David asked several girls to dance; they all accepted and seemed to enjoy dancing with him. Bert and Mary enjoyed the evening, dancing every dance, and were sorry when the night ended and the taxi returned to take them home. On the way they all said how they had enjoyed the evening out.

'How nice the ladies looked in their bright and colourful dresses,' said Mary, 'don't you agree David?'

'Certainly,' he replied, 'the bright blues, greens and yellows were lovely and a sight to behold and remember.' But to David not a girl at the dance looked as lovely or as attractive as Rosa had looked as she stood and played her violin for him in her red dress.

Over the next few months David went to more dances, and escorted some of the local girls home, but he never showed any interest in any of them, as they didn't match up to Rosa in his eyes.

Alfred returned home briefly on what he called "embarkation leave", and explained that he was going to serve overseas. He would be stationed in the Far East, probably in Singapore, as the RAF had a base there. He was looking forward to going; he enjoyed the Air Force, which was his life and gave him the opportunity to see more of the world. On his way home he had stopped off in London, to say goodbye to William, and had met his young lady.

The next few months passed quickly: David had been busy in the shop doing repairs and selling many new bicycles, as the weather had been good, which had helped trade. Employment in the neighbourhood was high and people had more money to spend on articles like bikes.

The situation, however, was not so good in many countries across mainland Europe. Political troubles had encouraged the rise of fascist dictators, who craved power and were beginning to invade neighbouring countries. The British Prime Minister had returned from Germany and declared that the document he held in his hand guaranteed "peace in our time", which reassured a nervous British population, anxious about the prospect of war.

Bert said that he never wanted to see another great conflict, as he did not want any of his sons to have to endure what he and his friends had had to suffer in the Great War.

One day, while in town, David called in to see Mr and Mrs Levine. He opened the door of the shop, and as Mr Levine looked up from what he was doing his eyes lit up when he saw David. Half turning to the inside door he shouted, 'Momma, Momma look who is here,' and with that he was round to where David was standing, shaking his hand. Almost immediately Mrs Levine was by his side and she hugged and kissed him like he was a long lost son. 'How are you David?' she asked.

Question after question followed this as they caught up with what he had been doing recently. When he finally got round to asking after Rosa he was told she was fine. She wrote fairly often to them and was enjoying Paris and her studies. Her tutor was old, but the best and was very kind; as were the people she was living with. She had asked her parents to pass on her kind regards to David if they saw him in the future, and they did. Before he went they also told David that she had met a fellow Jewish musician in Paris.

Just before he left Mr and Mrs Levine, David unbuttoned the top of his shirt and showed the St Christopher medallion that they had given to him. They all laughed and he told them it had been there since the day they had given it to him, and there it would stay. David said his goodbyes and was soon on his way. He liked Rosa's parents and believed that the feeling was mutual.

Since learning that Rosa had a male friend in Paris, David tried to put her to the back of his mind. He went to the occasional dance and took one or two local girls to the pictures, and enjoyed their company, but none of the girls became important to him. Mary and Bert agreed that time was on David's side, and that one day he would find Miss Right.

Alfred wrote home to tell them that he had been stationed in Singapore, and said that the sunshine and weather were marvellous and that he was enjoying his new life on the other side of the world.

On the third of September 1939, the dreaded news was announced that England was at war with Germany. Little did anyone envisage the global consequences of such news, and the change it would make to so many people's lives.

During the first few months of the war, there was very little conflict and many referred to it as the 'phoney war'. Britain mobilised but very little happened. Early in 1940 William wrote home to say that, like Alfred, he was going to volunteer and join the Air Force. He hoped that he would be selected to train for aircrew and as a result had put his wedding plans on hold. When Mary read this letter she was very unhappy at the thought of William being aircrew, and having to postpone the wedding; Bert was also very worried but tried not to show it.

As a result of the war David was very busy, everyone cycled more as petrol was rationed, therefore many cars were kept off the roads. Eventually cycle parts became harder to obtain, which made his job more difficult, but luckily many of the old bicycle parts that he had saved over the years now came in useful. Bert and the men in the town were working many hours each week, as industries like shipbuilding together with munitions and airplane factories, which were now supplying the war effort, took priority.

Mary and Bert kept up to date with news through the newspapers and wireless. They learnt about how the enemy had broken through the allies' defences, and how most of the British Army had escaped at Dunkirk. As a result most of the continent was now occupied, and the English people realised that this war was going to be more serious and that things were going to be very difficult and dangerous for everyone.

David knew he would have to serve his country, and so like his brothers he decided not to wait for call up and volunteered, however unlike his brothers he chose the Army. When he knew the date of his enlistment he tidied up his shop: all his new cycles had long since been sold, all his repairs had been completed, and the few remaining spare parts were greased and put in boxes in the shed on the allotment, ready for the day when the war finished and he could resume his business.

Before he went, David wished to say goodbye to Mr and Mrs Levine. When he visited them he couldn't help but notice a change in them: each had aged so much, and it was then that he realised that Rosa was under enemy occupation in Paris, and that she was a Jew. He had heard terrible things happening to Jews on the continent, and began to feel sick in his stomach at the thought of her being alone in France. Mr and Mrs Levine had not received any news from Rosa since the fall of France, and they were both desperately worried for her safety. They thanked David for calling, wished him luck in his new life and hoped for his safe return in the near future.

As he walked home his mind went back to Rosa, he had not thought about her much since he had learnt that she was seeing someone in France, but now he realised the danger she might be in, and it changed the whole perspective of his thinking, and he was very worried for her well being.

Soon the day came for David to leave home and join the Army. As he walked to the station to catch the train, like both his brothers before him, he wondered if he would be away for long, and if things and places would change much in his absence. The train was on time, he managed to find a seat, which was not easy anymore as trains were usually full of service personnel on leave. It was now that he realised that he was no longer a civilian, and would soon have to obey orders and get used to a new way of life, one so very different to what he had been used to, where he had been his own master.

The train made many stops picking up new recruits, before reaching its final destination; no sooner had David alighted on to the platform than a very loud voice shouted, 'All new recruits fall in on the platform.' David noticed that there was no "please", and it was at that moment that he realised he was in the Army. The men and boys soon did as they were told, and when their names had been checked on the roll call they were marched away to the camp under the watch of their NCO. David and the new recruits were soon housed and fed, (although he wasn't impressed with the food), but within time he would get acclimatised to the way of life and learn to obey orders at the double.

David soon adapted to his new Army life: somehow he didn't mind the discipline and orders and worked hard. He took pride in his uniform, the shine on his boots was brighter than the rest of the new recruits, and the effort he put in had been noticed by the NCOs and the officer in charge.

During his initial training, David excelled in everything:

drill, firearms, map reading, driving - he enjoyed the challenge that the Army presented to him. At the end of his initial training he was asked if he would like to be considered for special training that would involve a different type of commitment from the usual day to day routine he had experienced so far. He was given a little time to think it over, and was asked to let the Commanding Officer know as soon as possible. It didn't take David long to reach a decision and he soon requested an interview with the Commanding Officer, and said he would like to be considered for special training if possible.

The officer smiled and said, 'Yes, by all means. I guess you don't know what you have let yourself in for, but I wish you every success and luck in the future wherever you go.'

David stood back, saluted and left the room. It was then that he wondered what he had let himself in for, and he began to appreciate the old saying, "Never volunteer for anything in the army."

Back at home Mary was like a fish out of water: she had none of her sons to look after and Bert was working so much overtime that she saw very little of him. She missed calling at David's shop when she was in town, to do the bookkeeping and tidying up. The house seemed so quiet now, when William and Alfred had left it had made a big difference, but now that David had finally gone, she felt so alone and her life felt emptier than it had ever done since she first got married. The thought of her lads in the forces, and in so much danger, was a heavy weight on her mind that she could never forget. She wrote very often to them all and they in their turn were all very good at answering her letters and reassuring her of their safety.

William had been accepted for aircrew, and was now two thirds of the way through his course. When he got leave he secretly notified David, who organised leave to co-ordinate with his brother's so that they could surprise their Mother and go home together.

72

As they walked home from the station, the topic of conversation between the two brothers was very varied. They smiled and acknowledged everyone they knew, and also some that they didn't know; war really made a difference to people who respected the men in the services who were fighting and risking their lives for them. When they passed the allotment they stopped near Bert's shed and stood for a moment or so in silence. They found the key, unlocked the door, and gazed in, the shelves were still holding the bicycle spares in boxes where David had placed them and it was evident that nothing had been touched since he had left it. In the middle of the shed, taking up the most room, was David's cart. When William saw this his face broke out into a huge grin, 'You and your cart, our kid,' he said, 'Mum wrote to me and told me how you had progressed from barrow boy to cycle shop owner, and were doing quite well until this bloody war came about. You never did play like us kids when we were growing up, you were always on the look out to earn a few bob, and Ma said you never wasted a penny. Good luck to you young 'un, I guess, this war has put a stop to you in that direction for now, but if you survive, maybe you will continue to prosper when you are out of uniform. I hope you do.'

They soon left the shed, locked the door and continued on their walk. It was not long before the topic of the female sex cropped up. William said that his girlfriend in London had wanted to get married but he had dissuaded her for the time being. He knew that he possibly would start flying on operations, which were dangerous and from which many aircrew were lost. It was the thought of this that had prompted them to have sex before marriage, but he had taken every precaution, as he did not want to leave her in the family way when he left.

'Mum told me you were once interested in a Jewish girl, but she didn't think anything would come of it as the Jews never marry outside of their faith. She said that she'd gone abroad, and that you didn't see her nowadays.'

David shrugged off the comment, and did not expand on how he and Rosa had met, or on his meeting with the Levines. He quickly changed the subject, and said that he had been to quite a lot of dances, and met many girls, but so far had not been as fortunate as William in finding Miss Right. He thought that time was still on his side, and that when he had sex he would take care as William had done.

At this they gave a huge laugh, 'aren't we good boys,' they exclaimed, 'but I guess we had not let Mum hear us talking like this, she would never condone such talk, would she?'

Mary had managed to prepare them a grand meal, especially considering that most food was being rationed. She had saved what she could before they came.

When they all sat down at the table she said, 'I wish our Alfred was here to complete my family circle. Never mind we'll have a really good party when this horrid war is over and we are all together again. If we are still rationed I'll save as much as I can for weeks before, so that we can have a banquet.'

Bert shook his head when he heard her last remark and looked at his sons, 'Now that you two lads are away this is the kind of talk I have to put up with,' he said with a laugh, 'but I still love her and wouldn't swap her for the world. Anyway look at me, who else would have me?'

The meal was enjoyed at a leisurely pace, afterwards the boys helped Mary do the washing up and put the dishes and plates away in their respective places. Mary started work on the dirty laundry that the boys had brought home, and it was soon washed, ironed and ready for their departure, which came all too quick for the briefly reunited family.

CHAPTER 9

WHEN THE TIME CAME for the boys' departure they both hugged and kissed Mary at the front of the house. It was made a little easier for them when a group of girls who were passing wolf whistled and shouted, 'Can we get into line?'

The boys turned and shouted back, 'Yes please.' This was something that neither the boys nor the girls would have done before the war started, thought Mary as she waved them goodbye. David and William were catching trains in opposite directions from the station, so didn't travel together. William had a few more days leave and was going to see his girlfriend, Kathleen, whereas David was due back to camp, where he would begin his special training.

The war had now progressed into its second year, and seemed to be spreading and including more nations with each coming month. Air raids became more frequent, particularly on coastal areas where the seaports were. Mary and Bert's hometown, was an inland port, and had not had as many air raids as the coastal ports, and very little damage had been done, which all the local folk were pleased about.

When the Japanese bombed Pearl Harbour and the Americans entered the war, it gave the British people more hope, and made them feel that they were not fighting the enemy alone.

When David arrived back at the camp, many of those who had been on their initial training with him had left for their new units. Only David had been selected for the special training, and he knew that wherever he was sent he would go alone. The next day he got clearance from the camp, and was transported with all his kit, to the railway station. His rail ticket sent him to the top of Scotland, to an uninviting station that he had never heard of. He got off the train and asked the ticket collector if there was any transport to the Army camp.

The man replied, 'Aye man. The transport is here, it's your

feet, and it's straight on up the hill for five miles, you can't miss it. Them at the camp never send any transport unless it is for something very heavy, and I don't suppose your kit qualifies as something heavy do you?'

David was about to say, 'If you had to carry this lot for five miles I guess you would say it was classed as something heavy,' but thought that discretion was the better part of valour in this instance. Thanking the man, he picked up his kit and set off down the road and up the hill. Never had five miles seemed so long and he was pleased that it was not a blazing hot day. The physical exercise he had done in the basic training certainly helped him now, as he was far fitter than when he had originally joined the army. Little did David know that carrying his kit today was child's play and was nothing compared to what was in store for him in his future training at the camp. As he walked David kept stopping and having a rest, several Army lorries passed, but none stopped, even though he was in Army uniform. He wondered why he was being ignored by his so-called Army mates whom he had not yet met.

When he reached the camp he asked the guard where he should report. He was told where the orderly room was situated, and that there would be someone on duty, even though it was getting late for the orderly staff to be on duty. The junior NCO in the orderly room told him where his new billet was and gave him a pass for a meal in the mess hall after checking his travel warrants and making sure that everything was in order. Once he found the hut he was allocated to a very tired David put his kit on the only empty bed, paid a visit to the very clean toilet block, and then found the cookhouse, as he was very, very hungry.

The soldier on duty seemed a little bit friendlier and more talkative than the guard on duty. 'Hungry mate?' he asked. 'We don't run a four or five star restaurant here as you will soon find out, but I'll try and fill that stomach for now.'

He was correct when he said it was not five star food, but

David was thankful for anything that was available to eat there and then. When he finished his meal, the cook came over to have a chat with him. As they were alone he offered David a cigarette, which David refused. David explained that he had just finished his basic training and that he was now joining a special unit and asked if the cook was part of the new unit.

'No not me,' replied the cook, 'I'm on loan to those clowns, from the catering corp. I'm too old for what they train to do. I dare say that quite a lot of those that start the course will never finish it. You seem quite sane, so what are you doing here young fellow?' he asked with a laugh.

'I'm beginning to ask myself the same question,' answered David, 'and I've only just arrived.'

'The NCOs and the officers I'm sure are insane, the things they expect the men to do: climb cliffs and chimney stacks, be deep sea divers, swim rivers in full uniform with their boots and small packs on, and I mean real rivers, not just streams. They make them go on the moors, and live off the land for days with hardly any food. I think they're as mad as March hares, but I admit the CO never expects them to do anything he won't do himself, and he's no teenager. Like me, he lost those teenage years long ago. I hope I haven't upset you for a start, but it is as well to put you in the picture of what you are about to get from now on my lad.'

David thanked the cook and made his way back to the hut, which was to be his home from now on. It was still empty and David thought it rather peculiar that he had not seen many Army personnel about the camp since he arrived. He found a newspaper, laid it at the foot of the bed to put his feet up on, and was soon asleep.

How long he slept he did not know, but it did not seem to be long enough for him, as he was soon awoken by many feet tramping into the room and loud voices which seemed to be complaining.

'Hello, who have we got here then?' asked a loud voice.

At the same time he got a poke in his ribs from the person who was asking the question.

Before David could answer, the chap had sat down on the next bed to him. 'I'm Private David Jones,' David replied and as of yet I don't know which branch of the army I am in. Could you help me please?'

'You are in the crazy gang I should say,' came the reply, 'to do what we're expected to do you must be crazy, no not crazy, just sheer bloody mad, don't you agree chaps?' he asked turning to the rest of the men in the room.

The answer was a resounding "Yes" from every one of the men; it was then that David realised that the cook had not been joking. Everything that he had been told about the camp was true, as he was soon to find out.

It appeared that not all of the men were Army personnel, and that many were from the Navy and the Air Force. The Navy lads were Marines, and the Air Force lads were from the newly-formed Army of the RAF regiment, the rest were from many different branches of the Army. This diverse group of service men would all be under one command: if at sea the Navy took charge, if in the air the RAF and if on the ground the Army. Everyone was in Army uniform, and as of yet they had no shoulder badge, but one would be issued at a later date, which would include all three services.

Although David found the training hard from the start he was determined to stay the course. The esprit de corps among the chaps was marvellous, even the NCOs, although very strict were fair. Being an independent unit, each and every one had a job to do to make the unit a success, which it eventually was after many months of extensive training. Very few failed the course, though some had to leave through physical accidents that occurred during the demanding training.

Throughout his training David changed very much in appearance: his shoulders became broader, his complexion became darker and he developed muscles that he never knew he had.

When the training came to an end, the Commanding Officer called all the men on parade to inform them that they had an extra seven days leave starting immediately. He expected to see everyone back, on parade in exactly a week's time. When they were told of the leave most of the men thought that they would soon be posted overseas, as this was usually the case when extra leave was granted. The men soon left the camp anxious to make the most of their leave. David quietly slipped away, caught the train and went straight home.

When he got home, Mary could not believe the change that she saw in David, the harsh life he had been living had certainly not done him any harm and he seemed to have altered so much. Mary told David that the air raids had become more frequent than they used to be, and the bombs did not always land on the docks as intended, and as a result some civilians had been killed and houses destroyed.

The seven days leave was soon over and this time Mary walked with David to the station to see him off. Both hugged each other more fondly and longer than they had ever done, before David entered the railway carriage.

'Take good care of yourself son,' she remarked.

'And you too Mum,' he said as he waved her goodbye as the train pulled away from the platform.

All of the men who had been on leave were back on parade exactly seven days after it had been granted, as none dared disobey the CO's orders. He said that during the next few days the training would become more intensified and they would be expected to work harder than ever.

Back in the huts, the men discussed amongst themselves what course of action they would be involved in, and many thought that it would be a secret mission. They had all been confined to the camp for quite a few days, and were told that no mail would be allowed to be posted until they were notified that they could do so.

Eventually the day they had been waiting for arrived. They were soon summoned on to parade, and ordered to load ammunition and equipment on to lorries, and then they themselves jumped on a lorry and were on their way.

Their first stop was an aerodrome where they were loaded onto a large plane, which took off almost immediately. Their CO told them that until the plane landed again the pilot was to be their CO and they were to obey his orders.

'Hope the pilot doesn't tell me to jump,' said one of the soldiers, 'I ain't got a parachute sir, and although we had a budgie at home and I taught it to swear it never taught me to fly.'

'That's enough of that talk Watson,' shouted the senior NCO.

The Commanding Officer answered with a laugh, 'I admire humour such as that in these circumstances, I think it's very necessary and appropriate.'

The plane flew from Scotland to the south of England. It didn't fly too high, and as it was daylight the men got a good panoramic view of the countryside, no doubt they would have enjoyed the view far more if it had been peacetime and they had all been going on a holiday. Many wondered whether they would return from wherever they were going and whether this would be their last view of England. After an uneventful flight the plane touched down on an airfield near the south coast, it landed very smoothly and the men soon vacated the plane. Transport was waiting for them, and they were soon on their way to a port.

The senior NCO paraded the men on the quayside so that the Commanding Officer could address them and give them their orders. He began by saying that their next journey would be by sea, as they were going for a ride in a submarine courtesy of the Marines. Their mission would take them to a small island off the coast of Norway, on which was situated a weather and information centre, which had been captured by the enemy. They would land in darkness in small inflatable boats, leave time charges on fuel dumps and buildings in order to cause as much damage and consternation with as few casualties as possible. The men were informed that the island was heavily fortified, and that it wouldn't be an easy undertaking.

'I don't want any heroics from any of you, do you understand?' he concluded. 'We have trained long and hard for such a job as this, and as a team we will make a success of it. Good luck to each of you and take care.'

The senior NCO dismissed the parade when the CO had finished speaking to the men. Very soon they boarded the submarine which was to transport them and their weapons and explosives to their appointed destination.

They had not been on the submarine long when one of the chaps said, 'Now I know how a sardine feels when he is inside a tin laid alongside his brothers and sisters. It's a wonder the sailors living and working aboard these things are not deformed with the space that they have.'

Such humour as this had certainly helped them in the past months of long and tiring training, and it was very welcome now as it helped relax the tense atmosphere amongst the men. Whilst on board they were well fed, and were given a chance to rest as best they could in these cramped conditions. The submarine would surface as near to the shoreline as possible, and the men would then use inflatable boats to transport them to the island.

It was a very dark night and allowed the men to leave the submarine without being seen. As they rowed towards the shore the submarine soon descended to the deep, and the men knew they were now alone, and the sooner the job was done the better.

They all safely made it to the shore where they hid their boats amongst some rocks and marked them so that they could make a speedy retreat. The raiders had painted their faces black and wore dark overalls in order to help conceal their presence. They moved as silently as shadows, once again luck seemed to be on their side for the guards had no dogs with them on patrol that night which was a great asset to them.

When the guards moved further along the perimeter, the wire was cut on the fence, which once again helped as it was not wired up to the guardroom, or to any system which gave a warning. The invaders moved swiftly in placing their charges, it seemed almost like child's play, and almost unbelievably easy until one of the guards saw a shadow move, and immediately gave a warning.

With that a huge searchlight next to an anti aircraft gun swung into action, and the whole of the compound was swathed in a very bright light making it seem like daylight. Machine guns were firing from every direction and chaos, that no training could have prepared the men for, was all around. David seemed to be the one nearest to the searchlight, and decided to do something about it. Taking the pin from a grenade he ran towards the light, and threw it at the gun. Almost immediately the lamp was extinguished much to the relief of his comrades. Almost before he realised what a risk he had taken, the time charges that had been set to go off at intervals started to blow up the fuel stores, vehicles and the tower that housed so much valuable equipment - nothing was spared. There was so much confusion in the camp, which allowed the raiders to make a successful retreat.

One or two had been wounded in the exchange of fire, but none appeared to be life threatening. The light caused by so many explosions was like Dante's inferno, flames and explosions everywhere causing rage, terror and no doubt flight to those trying to extinguish and curb further explosions. None of the enemy seemed bothered in trying to capture the raiders, and very few shots were exchanged by either side, as they were trying to save as much of the island camp as possible.

The men found their boats with ease, and were soon on the sea and waiting at their prearranged meeting point to be picked up by the submarine. The sea covers a large area, so it was no surprise when there was no submarine to be seen and soon seeds of doubt were set in the men's minds as to whether it would appear. Someone said the Navy lads could not be on time to meet a bird at a bus stop and that he did not feel like rowing all the way back to England. After a few minutes, which seemed like hours the submarine surfaced not too far away, and they were soon safe and warm on board.

The sub contained a medical officer who soon attended to the wounded men. The Captain said he had put the conning tower up and witnessed the explosions, so he knew that the mission had been a success. However he had had to submerge soon after as he saw enemy war ships nearby and this was the reason for his delay in returning to pick up the raiders.

Back at the camp in Scotland, the CO thanked his men for a job well done and informed them that they would continue training for similar raids in the future. There would be more hit and run raids with more personnel and then one day maybe a huge invasion to liberate Europe. When he had finished talking to his men, he said he wanted a private word with David. David spent what time he had on spit and polish in order for his interview with his CO and wondered what could be in store for him. Little did he know that what he was about to hear would haunt him for the rest of his life.

When he was shown into the CO's room he saluted and stood to attention. The CO dismissed the NCO who had escorted David into the room and gave the order to stand at ease.

'Firstly I want to say something about the way you put that searchlight out of action. I know that you acted swiftly, and no doubt it saved us quite a lot of casualties, and for that I want to thank you, but in future no more heroics. Here we work together as a team as we have been trained to do. Anyway I am going to promote you, from today you have your first stripe, and knowing you I doubt it will be long before you have another to go with it.'

The CO sat down and a changed look came over his face, and the tone of his voice changed, 'Jones, I'm afraid it is my duty to inform you of the death of your mother and father.

They were both killed in an air raid in your hometown. From what I can gather the whole street where they lived was destroyed, not a wall was left standing and there were no survivors. Please accept my deepest sympathy. I have arranged a short leave for you to visit your hometown and make any necessary arrangements. If I can be of any further assistance, please don't be afraid to contact me. You are now dismissed Jones.'

David saluted and left the room. So much had happened and his whole world had been turned upside down in such a short space of time that he could hardly take it in, he felt as if someone had kicked him hard in his stomach.

CHAPTER 10

IN PARIS, Rosa kept on the move, never staying long in any one given place. She had cut short her long black hair and had dyed it blonde. She had started to use much lighter shades of makeup in order to make herself look less Jewish. As a girl at school she had learnt French, and since living in France she had passed as a French woman.

She had managed to get false identification papers and food cards, and managed to earn enough to live by playing her violin in cafes and restaurants. So far she had been lucky to stay clear of trouble, and had avoided being rounded up as many Jews had been, who then disappeared. She began to focus on surviving this bad period and looking for a way to get back home to England and her parents. She had not heard from her old tutor for quite some time, and often wondered what had become of him. She was too frightened to try and contact him, for it was hard to know who you could trust.

She had so very few possessions, as she was limited to what she could cram into a suitcase and carry easily from place to place along with her violin. She was thankful that she was living in a place as large and busy as Paris, as she could mingle in with the crowds and become anonymous and not arouse suspicion in any way.

She played in cafes and restaurants to both French and German audiences, who seemed to like and appreciate her music. Playing before German officers filled her with revulsion, though she never dared show it, and it was probably this brave face that had helped her stay free for so long. The money that she earned and the tips that she received paid for her accommodation, bought her food and a few items of clothing in which to keep up her appearance.

Rosa managed to survive in this manner for quite a long while until one day someone exposed the lie she was living and reported her. She was taken to the German headquarters for questioning where she learnt that she had been under surveillance for quite sometime. At the end of her long and arduous questioning she was told that along with other 'Jewish scum', she would be transported from France in the near future, to a place that was only fit for such 'filth' as herself.

After this she was thrown into a cell where she spent the next twenty-four hours alone and frightened. Although it had a sink, a toilet and a bunk, the small dark cell provided little in the way of comfort. She had no change of clothes as she had been arrested when she left the café where she had been playing, so all she had with her was her violin. As she washed herself in the sink she noticed the St Christopher medallion and chain, she took it from around her neck, wrapped it in her handkerchief and wedged it in the bottom of the violin so that it would not move and rattle. It was the only jewellery she had with her, and was very important to her as it represented memories of home, her parents and David.

With nothing to do but contemplate what might happen to her, the time went slowly for Rosa. Eventually around midnight, the cell door opened and she was ordered out and told she was about to go on a journey.

In the shadows at the back of the German HQ was a large covered van, into which she was thrown. Inside, in the half-light she could discern several figures, male and females with a few small children, all Jews, huddled together like frightened sheep. No one spoke as the door was closed behind her and the van drove away. The journey was not a long one, and eventually they reached a railway station in Paris where freight and goods were handled. Stationed in a long row were a number of covered rail wagons, all with their big doors open and nothing inside.

As the van came to a halt next to one of the wagons, the doors were opened, and the occupants told to get out and line up. A German officer checked their names against a list and were told to climb into the empty dark wagons. Being quite high from the ground, one or two of the men climbed inside first and helped the rest up. Before long more covered vans came into the freight yard and discharged their loads of people under armed guards. More and more people were loaded into Rosa's wagon until it was uncomfortably crowded. When no more vans arrived and all the wagons were full of their human cargo, the doors were slammed shut, an engine attached and the train sent on its way.

There was so little room for the people squashed together on the straw covered floor, and a silence fell over the wagon as no-one knew how long they would be confined to the trucks or how far they would travel. When people decided to talk to one another, the only conversation was why had they been rounded up in the middle of the night and put into these wagons to be taken heaven knows where. After quite sometime travelling and no toilet facilities in the wagon the men decided that all the straw on the floor should be pushed into one corner of the truck in a pile to serve as a toilet. The edges were trampled down so as to soak up any seepage, and when the women wanted to relieve themselves the men would form a wall with their backs to the woman to give her a modicum of privacy.

After hours of travel the train eventually stopped, shunted into sidings and eventually the doors were slid back. The guards arrived carrying buckets of water with ladles and chunks of rye bread in cardboard boxes, which were placed just inside the trucks. They said some carts would be available before the train left so if they wanted to clear out the soiled straw and empty it into the carts then they could do so, more straw would then be made available. The only reason they were doing this was because the Germans did not want their trucks contaminated by 'Jewish filth'. No one was to be allowed to leave the inside of their trucks, anyone doing so would be shot. It was a good job that the time of year was fairly mild for if it was winter most of the occupants would have been frozen stiff by now.

The stench and atmosphere in these trucks was almost

unbelievable, and once the door was shut there was hardly any light inside, some boards at the top of the truck had been taken off and steel bars placed instead to make them more secure, but these gave more fresh air and light to the inside of the truck.

The journey seemed to take several days and in such cramped conditions it was a horrible nightmare. The occupants were of all ages: young, middle aged, old with quite a few children, who seemed to cry most of the time through fear and hunger. Rosa was frightened too, but more than thankful in the knowledge that her parents were safe and sound in England and that she was single and had not got any children to console and care for.

Eventually the train came to a halt with a huge jolt almost throwing its passengers on top of each other. After what seemed like an age the wagon doors were thrown wide open and in the daylight they could see their destination. In front of them was a huge camp with many huts and huge buildings; high fences could be seen surrounding the perimeter, inside seemed to be hundreds of inmates, everyone of them – men, women and children dressed in the same drab, striped coat and trousers. A few had caps on but those that did not appeared to have had their heads shaved.

Army guards were everywhere, and most had a huge snarling guard dog held on a lead, which could easily be freed to attack on a given command from its handler. The inmates of the wagons, who had just arrived at the camp, were lined up, checked and marched away by the guards to some empty huts, whose dogs snarled and tried to attack the new inmates as they passed. The sight and sound of these huge beasts filled Rosa with fear and she immediately thought of the time when David had saved her from the dog attack years ago, but there was no David to come to her aid now.

When she first saw the inmates of the camp Rosa noticed how frail and ill they looked. She thought they were suffering from malnutrition and she was soon to discover why. The huts she and the other new arrivals were allocated to were no better than the wagons which had brought them here, in fact they were worse, for they had been used longer and had housed so many inmates, who had passed through the camp. They contained rows of bunk beds, which had been roughly constructed from planks of wood with a wire mesh frame on which to lie. A few had filthy mattresses, but most had only a layer of straw and most of this seemed to have fallen onto the floor which was made of concrete. There were not many windows to give light and ventilation, only a few tables and stools and that was it. The washrooms and toilets were no better, and the state of hygiene everywhere was deplorable.

The next day the entire room was ordered to a fairly large building, where they were told to strip off all their clothes. Next their hair was shorn off with electric clippers, and then they were issued with the striped tops and trousers that everyone else seemed to wear. The food that they were given was very poor and meagre: mainly poor soup and black rye bread, which never seemed to appease the pangs of hunger.

In less than a week Rosa was taken from the hut, to an almost empty room, except for a table, some chairs and a large bath of what looked like very cold water. In the room there were six large heavy men in uniform, looking very stern and anything but pleasant. She was told that they thought she was a British spy. They said that they knew she could speak English, Russian and French and that her parents were from Russia. She was told that she was to be interrogated and it would be to her advantage if she told what she knew. She said that she was no spy, but had come to France to further her violin playing and could tell them nothing.

Next she was told to strip naked; knowing that it was useless to argue with six strong men she obeyed their command. A table was pushed back and she stood there in front of them, one took off his leather belt and if she failed to answer a question he would beat her on her legs and buttocks. As she had nothing to tell, she was unable to answer their questions and she was whipped with the belt. She screamed with pain, and when again no answers were forthcoming, cigarettes were stubbed out on her naked body. Next she was plunged into the ice-cold bath, this almost stopped her breath but momentarily stopped her screams and yells. She was placed on a tabletop, and when electric shocks were administered to her body she gave out one huge long scream and passed into unconsciousness, she could take no more. The men who were holding her on the table released their grip and she hardly moved a nerve. One said she either knows nothing or she is a very brave woman, and I think it is the former. Someone was called in to dress her, which was not easy as she was so limp and lifeless.

The men departed and she was left in the room alone, she lay there a long time and then she gradually came to. The beatings, the burns, the water and last the amount of electricity administered had taken its toll on her, and it was a marvel she had survived. As she laid there for what seemed like hours, her only thoughts were why should these men want to hurt and maim so many helpless people. As far as she could remember she had never wanted to hurt anyone in her whole life, and as for secrets she knew nothing.

The door opened and a couple of people came into the room, and with great difficulty helped her off of the table and almost had to carry her back to her hut, such was the beating that had been inflicted upon her. They did not take her very far into the hut, but left her in a crumpled heap on the floor, some of her roommates helped her onto her bed. Luckily her beloved violin was still laid on the corner of her bed. It was her only possession, but at that moment of time she was so traumatised to even care about it. Within time most of the bruising went but the burn marks would remain with her throughout her life as evidence of what had been inflicted upon her.

When the inmates of the huts were moved they never returned, and she sometimes wondered what had happened to them. There was always a horrid smell hanging over the camp, and many rumours went round that it was the smell of burnt flesh.

When she was recovering, one of the guards noticed the violin case and asked if she could play. She said yes and was told to report to a certain room, as the Camp Commandant wanted an orchestra made up of inmates to play whilst the officers took their evening meal.

They certainly looked a motley band of musicians standing there playing in the dining room, their heads shaved, dressed in the limp striped clothes that hung on the emaciated figures. The only advantage was that it was warmer in winter and cooler in summer standing playing there, but the sight of those men and a few women feasting themselves on food, immaculately laid out on tables, nearly drove the poor starving musicians insane. There was nothing they could do about it, the only consolation they had was that while they were playing they were still alive.

So far, she had not been sent for any further interrogations or beatings, which undoubtedly would be the end of her. How she had kept her sanity she did not know, her looks had gone, as had her figure and her once lovely image had been transformed into a malformed frame of skin and bone. She was one of thousands in the camp who looked the same. Many was the time that she thought how fortunate it was that she had been taught to play the violin, as it was being able to play and entertain that kept her alive. She prayed for a day when things would change, but how, she could not imagine, and she prayed that she didn't disappear like most of the other inmates.

CHAPTER 11

ONCE HIS CO had dismissed him, David swiftly left the camp in a daze and made his way to the railway station. The train could not take him home quick enough to see what had happened to his parents and home. It was a different home coming to what he was generally used to: this time there was no loving parents to greet him, not even a house to give him shelter. It was then he realised that from now on his life would never be the same again.

As he walked from the station to where he once lived, he met several people whom he knew. They all offered him their condolences, and were so very sorry for him. He was grateful to them, as he then realised that his parents had been well-respected members of the community, which helped him a lot.

When he reached the place where his home once stood he could hardly believe what he saw: from end to end the whole street had been devastated into one huge mound of bricks, rubble and glass. Nothing had been spared, and no living thing could have survived underneath.

As he stood motionless, looking at the devastation, he suddenly felt a hand on his shoulder and a voice saying, 'Its hard for you lad isn't it? But there is one consolation, no-one suffered and it was all over in a flash.'

David did half a turn and immediately recognised one of his mother's old friends who had gone to school with her. As she did not live too far away, they had kept in touch. They had much in common as they had married and brought up families in similar circumstances over the years.

'Hello Mrs Thomas,' said David, 'I was just thinking about the past. I've not been here long; I just came from the station. I came as quick as I could to see what had happened and to do what I can.'

'I notice you have your small pack hanging from your shoulder and now you have no home to stay in. I guess you had better come and stay with me until you return to camp. I know our Tom won't mind you having his bed. He's in the forces now and is serving overseas, so he won't be wanting it for a while, and the rest of the family are married and have moved away from home. It'll be nice to have someone to talk to; Mr Thomas is working so many hours on war work that I hardly see him these days, and when I do he's too tired to talk.'

David thanked Mrs Thomas for her hospitality, and as he had nowhere else to go was more than thankful to accept her kind offer.

Both stood there looking at the carnage when Mrs Thomas said, 'Come on lad, time we made a move. I reckon you could do with a nice cup of tea, and we can't do any good standing here.'

They soon reached Mrs Thomas house, which was like Mary's had been before the bomb devastated it. She soon produced a pot of tea along with a biscuit, and warmly said, 'Make yourself at home David, because until you go back this is your home.'

David felt comfortable and relaxed and when Mr Thomas arrived home from work, he too made him feel welcome. Mrs Thomas' son, Tom had a very comfortable bed, and although it had been a very traumatic and tiring day David was soon fast asleep.

The next day David visited the bank and the solicitor, and dealt with all the matters concerning his parents' death. When the bodies were eventually recovered which took some considerable time, they were buried in a communal grave, with the other victims of the bombing.

Whilst on his short leave, David visited some of his old friends and family. Finally he made his way to Mr and Mrs Levines' house. When he got there, their shop was closed, and the house appeared empty. He enquired of their whereabouts, but could only learn that they had left the area sometime ago.

David's short leave soon came to an end, and he thanked Mr and Mrs Thomas very much for their kind hospitality and consideration. As he shook Mrs Thomas' hand he gave her a hug and was very pleased to hear her say, 'What I have done for you, I know your mother would have done for any of my family should they have been placed in the same circumstances. From now on my home is your home should you need one. Good luck and take good care of yourself David.' She stood at the door waving to him until he was out of sight just as Mary had done so many times in the past.

The railway journey back to camp gave David more time to think as he sat in the carriage. Although it was full he felt alone, more so than he had ever felt in his entire life: his parents were now gone from him forever, Alfred was in the Far East and William was frequently flying on dangerous air raids. Then there was Rosa, was she still alive, and if so where? After all the reports of the Jews he had heard, maybe it would be as well for her own sake, if she had not survived. All these things seemed to flash through his mind at once, and it was a good thing that he soon reached his destination and had to alight from the train and make his way back to camp.

Next day David resumed his training, and a lot of this dark mood passed away from him. He trained harder and longer than he had ever done before and was soon promoted again, this time being awarded a second stripe. This meant that he had to move and was now stationed with different people. Although he was very young, they readily accepted his orders, which he gave with authority. He took part in a few more small nuisance raids, and thanks to David, his section always suffered very few casualties, which was no doubt due to the trust his men placed in him. If there was ever an element of danger in the missions he shouldered it himself if at all possible, and because of this he was well respected by his men.

When the men were due their next leave, one of David's pals Paul, who was the same rank, asked David where he was going to spend his leave now he had no home to go to.

'I was going to stop here,' replied David.

'I'm going to my sister's,' said Paul, 'would you like to come with me? I'm sure my sister won't mind if I take a guest for the week.'

He told David that his sister was a bit untidy. He would have to let her know that David was coming, as she would probably have to borrow some cups and maybe a bit of bedding from the neighbours. The kids were a bit unruly, but the dog didn't bite - well so far it had not bit him, and the cat usually kept off of the table at meal times. The pub was not too far from the house, and it was there that she was usually to be found.

David did not seem to be interested much in this invitation, as the mental picture he had built up of Paul's sister wasn't particularly inviting, but after a bit of persuasion he accepted in the expectation that it would not be quite as bad as his friend suggested.

The day for their leave soon arrived. It was May, and the weather was ideal for seven days holiday away from Army life. David and Paul were soon on their way to the station. Paul lived in a market town in a beautiful part of the country, as David was about to find out. When they arrived they walked through the town and on to a very poor dilapidated area where the houses would have been condemned had it not been for the war. David began to wish that he had refused the invitation if one of these slums was to be his home for the next week. As he was thinking this they stopped at a bus stop and almost immediately a bus pulled up. He followed Paul on to the bus, which left the town, and was soon out into the countryside. David loved the countryside and at this time of year it was looking its best.

The bus soon stopped at a green in a very pretty village, around which were a number of white cottages with well-kept gardens. Adjusting their webbing packs they set off to the home of Paul's sister. They stopped at the end of the village outside what David thought was a small hotel: at the end of the drive was a lovely house, which was situated in the middle of well kept gardens and lawns.

'Is this where you have brought me?' asked David in bewilderment.

'Well it's where my sister lives, so you had better come and meet her,' said Paul, and with that he started to walk up the drive to the front door.

Paul rang the bell and a woman answered the door. When she saw Paul she hugged and kissed him - it was easy to see the affection they had for each other. After a moment or two Paul introduced David to Nancy his sister. Nancy was quite a few years older than Paul; she was tall with a nice figure and good complexion, medium brown hair and a lovely smiling face.

'Come inside I have a snack ready for you both now and later we will have dinner,' said Nancy.

The wide entrance hall had quite a few rooms leading from it. The hall was very impressive with a delft rack holding Dutch plates, and a wide staircase leading upstairs. The décor, the carpets and furniture were all of the highest quality; in fact everything was in keeping with a home of this size, and not a thing was out of place.

When they had their snack, Nancy talked about her family, she had just one daughter almost as old as Paul and David, who was at university. Her husband was a medical doctor, who was away in the forces.

Nancy prepared the evening meal, and when David entered the dining room he saw the table all laid out. The cutlery and glasses shone as if they had been burnished, the china too seemed as though it had been designed for a setting such as this, all in all it looked perfect. Nancy apologised for the meagre meat course and said that tomorrow she would try and get some fish and poultry if possible, as they were not rationed as meat was. David thought he could have enjoyed a slice of bread and butter in such elegant surroundings.

When they were alone, David asked Paul why he had lied to him about his sister's circumstances.

'If I had told you the truth that you were coming to a home as nice as this, would you have come?' asked Paul.

'I doubt it very much,' answered David.

'Exactly. I knew you could do with a place to stay, and I knew that Nancy would make you very welcome; also it's company for her.'

When they all retired for the night, David lay in his bed, which was larger and more comfortable than any he had ever slept in before. He thought to himself, 'If I do survive this conflict and come out of it fit and well, I will have everything that is the best, like here in this house; no more back to back houses, those days will be gone forever. I realise that it won't be easy and yes, this crazy war is yet to end and I have to survive, in order to achieve such aims, but that is my aim in life,' and with that he fell into a deep sleep.

When he awoke, bright sunshine was pouring into the room. He had slept longer than he had intended, mainly due to the comfortable bed. When he had eaten breakfast he asked Nancy where Paul was.

'You won't see much of Paul for the next six days,' answered Nancy, 'there are still one or two of his old girlfriends who are not married, that he will want to see. There are also a lot of Land Army and service girls in this area, so he won't be lonely for long I'm sure. If you get tired of my company and want to follow suit, then I will understand. Your bed and meals will be here for you as normal, just as Paul's will be for him. If you have any washing whilst you are here, just give it to me and I'll do it for you.

David thanked Nancy and asked her if there was anything he could help her with.

'I'm going to tidy the garden and pick anything that is ready to eat from the vegetable patch, so you can help me with that if you like?'

Nancy and David worked together very well, and it was a

complete change to have a woman to talk to, for he did not have much contact with the opposite sex, nor did he seek it. When it became too hot to work in the garden, they sat in the shade and had a cool drink.

David continued to help Nancy with any jobs he could: drying the dishes, preparing vegetables, helping her as she went shopping. Throughout all these jobs they talked openly and freely, each finding the other's company very compatible.

As he put away some gardening tools, David noticed two bicycles in the shed. Taking them out, he quickly oiled and serviced them, and briefly thought about his shop before the war. Having tried and tested them he found Nancy in the kitchen and asked, 'Would you like to go for a ride in the countryside, seeing as though it's such a nice day? I'm not going to take no for an answer as I am sure that you can manage to spare an hour or two from your chores, because I have helped you with a lot of them.'

Nancy looked up from what she was doing and her face lit up. 'Oh David I would love to, its ages since I was on a bike, are the cycles OK?'

'Yes, I have seen to them and they are fine.'

Discarding what she was doing Nancy said, 'Give me ten minutes and I'll be ready. We'll leave a note for Paul should he call and wonder where we are. We're having a cold meal this evening so nothing will spoil.'

Nancy returned very soon from changing, she had put on a lovely thin, pale pink summer dress with sandals that matched. She had brushed her hair out and was smiling like a teenager on her first date. As she pushed the cycle before getting on it she looked so happy and carefree.

They were soon into the country and there was not a bit of traffic on the quiet country roads. It was hard to tell which of the two enjoyed the cycle ride the most. Nancy knew there were no shops or pubs where they were going, and as there was a basket on her handlebars she had brought a bottle of water in case they become thirsty. They soon needed a rest and stopped to admire the countryside around them, before heading home.

Paul was in the house when they returned and hoped that they had enjoyed their cycle ride. Someone had sold him some tickets for a dance that was to be held the following night, and he hoped that they would go with him, as it would be their last evening on leave. Both David and Nancy agreed and thanked him for the tickets.

The day of the dance was taken up with last minute chores. Nancy wanted to go to the hairdresser's before the dance, and the boys' uniforms required pressing so she had not a lot of spare time. The dance was held in the local village hall so people could walk there, which meant that it should be well attended.

Nancy said she and her husband had not attended a dance in a long time and she hoped that someone would ask her to dance, even if she only managed the one all evening. When the time came for them to leave and Nancy came down the stairs, Paul looked up at her and said, 'Our Nancy you have never looked so lovely, not even on your wedding day and you were much younger then.' Indeed he was correct for tonight it was hard to believe she had a grown up daughter.

'You always could try and butter people up our Paul, but it never got you far,' she said with a laugh.

David didn't say a word, but thought how beautiful she looked. When they went on the cycle ride she had looked so very beautiful, but tonight she looked so elegant, it was hard to describe her beauty. When they arrived, the dance was already in progress and the floor was fairly full. Once Nancy had returned from the cloakroom Paul walked over to her and asked her for a dance, 'I will see that you have one dance,' he said with a smile.

When the dance was over, he said with a grin, 'There, she's yours now,' as he returned Nancy to David.

When the next dance started David took Nancy on to the

floor. As he held her in his arms it was if she was floating on air, for never had she danced with a partner so free and easy and yet so safe and secure - they danced as if they were one. They had just finished a dance, and were waiting for the next to start, which was to be a waltz. The band started to play and David soon recognised the tune, he became stiff and tense and asked if they could sit this one out. The tune they were playing was "Fascination".

As Nancy looked at David she saw a change in his expression, she asked, 'Are you alright?'

'I'm fine let's dance, I love a waltz.'

She noticed that he seemed to hold her closer to him, and it was the same with every dance they shared after that. They danced together for the rest of the evening and never changed partners.

When the dance came to an end, Paul said that he was escorting his newfound lady friend home and that he would see them at the house later. Nancy had never enjoyed a dance more, even when she was courting her husband. He could dance, but not like David, and no one had ever held her like he had tonight.

It had been a marvellous evening, and they didn't hurry as they walked home. As there were not many people around at that time of night, they walked hand in hand. David briefly explained about Rosa, and how they had met and why he froze when he heard "Fascination" playing. Nancy said that she could feel the concern David felt for Rosa, and hoped that she was safe and well.

When they reached the driveway of the house they paused for a minute or two. David said he would like to thank her for the hospitality she had shown him for the past six days, and that he had enjoyed the evening immensely.

They were just about to start walking again when he asked her, 'Would be offended if I kissed you good night as a thank you for the marvellous evening?'

'Of course you may David,' she replied, 'I should have

been disappointed if you had not done so, for I have had a night to remember thanks to you.'

David took her in his arms and the kiss on her lips seemed to last for minutes as each seemed reluctant to end the embrace. When they did Nancy said, 'If I was much younger, single and free I am sure that I would try to rival Rosa, or any other female for your affection,' then she gave a small chuckle and a smile that David would remember for a long time.

The front door opened and Paul stood there, 'I thought I heard you coming up the drive,' he said, 'I've put the kettle on so we can have a drink before we go to bed. Enjoy the dance did you?' Then he answered his own question, 'I know you did, both of you. I'm pleased that I got the tickets for us, and Nancy, you were the belle of the ball.' They talked about the dance while they had their drinks and then retired to their respective bedrooms.

David could not sleep for some considerable time as thoughts of Nancy, her husband, the kiss, Rosa and the tune Fascination were all spinning through his mind. Here he was between two women, both of whom he loved and admired, but who he knew he could never have. Nancy was from a different world to him, and what's more was married to a husband who loved her and had a family. Rosa was from a different religion, one that never married out of their faith, and also he didn't know where she was or even if she was still alive.

Nancy laid on her bed very much awake. Since David came into her home only six short days ago, her whole life seemed to have taken on a new meaning. From tomorrow, Paul and David would say goodbye to her, her life would revert back to its normal pattern and routine, and she must try and forget the past six days. It would not be easy but she must succeed for everyone's sake not least her own. She was no longer a teenager and must put these flights of fancy behind her, which she was prepared to do, and be thankful that she was still desirable to a young man like David.

Next morning when the boys had taken their breakfast and were ready to go, Nancy held and kissed Paul. When she shook David by the hand, she gave it a little squeeze in a way that Paul didn't notice, and told them both to take good care of themselves. As they walked away David thought that it would have been better if Paul had taken him to a home and a Nancy as he had first described, but fate had a habit of deciding such things and he was happy that it had brought him to this Nancy.

CHAPTER 12

ON THE JOURNEY BACK to camp, Paul and David discussed the future and what they intended to do once the war was over. Paul said that he wanted to move to New Zealand; he had once spoken to an airman who had been a sheep farmer down there, and his description of the lifestyle and the weather had made a big impression on him.

'When this war comes to an end, if I'm still in one piece, I am seriously considering moving out there,' he said.

David said that since the bomb had fallen on his home and killed his family, he doubted if he would return to his hometown and resume his old lifestyle again. He said that he wanted much more from life than his parents had, and he would work hard to achieve it.

Before their conversation came to an end David asked Paul whether the photographs he had noticed in Nancy's hall were of her husband.

'Yes,' answered Paul. 'He's a surgeon, he used to work in the local hospital, but he's in the army now. I know he works very hard and I'm sure that a lot of people owe their lives to him. He's a grand fellow is Ted, very quiet, but he really loves our Nancy and his daughter.'

When they got back to the camp David wrote Nancy a short thank you letter. He just wanted to say how much he had enjoyed his short stay with her, and thanked her for the hospitality that she had shown him.

As they became more experienced, David and his squad were sent on more rigorous training exercises and night escapades along the south coast. Orders came through, and they were eventually sent on a mission to gather information about the German coastal defences in Northern France.

They were taken as near as possible to the French coast, where they were set adrift in canvas canoes to get closer to the coast, from where they would then have to swim, dragging the canvas boats behind them. They infiltrated the coastline at several points over a number of nights, without causing any suspicion. It was a hazardous and dangerous mission and they were told to try and escape injury and capture at all costs.

Most of the men on David's mission were single; such was the danger that married personnel were discouraged from going. David was pleased that he was not married, and that he could serve his country in such a way.

Thanks to the intense training and experience acquired on their past missions, the raid was a success. What they didn't realise was that their reconnaissance trips were to play a huge part in the future of the war, and that their observations would help in the liberation of Europe.

* * * * *

On June 6th 1944 a huge fleet set sail from the south coast of England bound for occupied France. David and his fellow soldiers were some of the first to land and lead the invasion; the fighting was fierce and many sacrificed their lives. Nancy's husband, Ted had come over with the Army Medical Corps and was extremely busy tending the casualties. Nancy knew that Paul, Ted and David would all be in the thick of the action, so she had three to worry about and pray for. Her prayers must have been answered for they all survived the first few days of the invasion.

Days turned into weeks, weeks into months, and the tide of battle seemed to have turned on the side of the allies. There had been heavy losses on both sides, but more were to come before the final victory was achieved in the late spring of 1945, when Germany surrendered.

Ted wrote regularly to Nancy; Paul wrote infrequently, and told her that he and David had been transferred to different units due to casualties and replacements, which meant she now had no news of David whatsoever. One day when her daughter was home from university for a few days, she saw the letter that David had written to Nancy thanking her for her hospitality.

'Who's this David, Mum? He's got neat writing and he writes a very nice letter of appreciation. Is he nice Mum?' Nancy gave one of her lovely smiles and answered, 'Very nice my love.'

Nancy didn't tell her daughter about how David had helped her do the garden or wash the dishes, nor she didn't tell her about the bicycle ride, the dance or the kiss, which was so freely given.

'He's just a young soldier that your Uncle Paul brought home on leave with him. He lost his home and parents in a bombing raid earlier this year and had nowhere to go.' She and David had done nothing wrong, and she had nothing to hide or be ashamed of, but she did not want to sow seeds of suspicion in her daughter's mind. She didn't want to lose any of the love or admiration that her daughter, whom she loved so much, had for her. She thought that she would probably never see or hear from David again and that their previous meeting would only be a sweet memory. Taking the letter from Jean's hand, she tore it up into shreds and placed it in the bin and continued with the housework.

The Army advanced across Europe, liberating cities, towns and villages. In the forest of the Belgian Ardennes, David and his men experienced the worst winter the local people had ever known. Temperatures had fallen well below freezing, and ice, snow and thick fog lasted for two weeks. The troops had not been equipped for such cold conditions, and this made their job more difficult and dangerous. The fog allowed the Germans to move their tanks and artillery in the dense forestation undetected, and as a result, they were advancing quicker than the allies expected and there were many casualties.

At around ten o'clock on the morning of December 25, the fog cleared, the sun broke through and the enemy were pushed back out of the woods and into the open countryside, where they were like ducks on a shooting range. The allied

Air Force mobilised quickly, and what seemed like hundreds of planes took to the air as the fog lifted; each carried rockets, which were soon fired on the defenceless enemy. If ever anything helped the situation, it was the good Lord's sun clearing the fog so the planes could take off. This battle became known as the Battle of the Bulge and was a major turning point in the war, and signalled the road to victory in Europe, in just a few short months.

David and some of his usual troop of men had been sent to the Ardennes from Holland where, together with many more troops, they were trying to stop the enemy advance before the fog cleared on Christmas Day. They were experienced soldiers and were immediately thrown into the most dangerous part of the ensuing battle. Before the day was out David and many of his men had been hit by shrapnel and needed hospital treatment. The wounded were placed in an ambulance and driven to the nearest field hospital, which was a requisitioned chateau a few miles from the front line.

The nurse who had admitted them immediately went to see the surgeon, and said, 'Half a dozen men have been brought in from the fighting; all are wounded and need attention. They are all from one unit, under the command of a young junior NCO, who is most insistent that they should all be seen to before himself'.

The surgeon examined the wounded straight away; one of the men's wounds was more serious than the others, and turning to the nurse he said, 'I don't think we can save his arm, I think we'll have to amputate. Get ready nurse.'

As he turned to leave the room he was stopped by David, who had overheard what he had said. 'Please sir, do not remove his arm, please try to save it, if ever a soldier deserves to leave the forces with his body intact it is him sir.'

He looked into David's eyes and was determined to try his hardest to save the arm. 'Young man,' he said, 'only the Lord works miracles but I will try and emulate the Lord in performing one today.' The surgeon worked hard, and after a few hours the operation was a success, and David was told that his man wouldn't lose his arm.

The medical team then attended to the rest of the wounded in the makeshift theatre. When everyone had been treated, the soldiers thanked them, and said it was unbelievable what they had done in such working conditions.

The next day, David, and those of his wounded mates who could be moved, were transferred to a hospital far from the fighting. After a few weeks convalescence their wounds healed, and David and his men were transferred back to their units. So many of the men had been killed and injured in the fighting that on his return David was promoted to sergeant.

The Battle of the Bulge had been more decisive than at first thought, as the allied troops advanced and now were fighting on the enemy's home soil. As each day dawned it became more apparent that the war in Europe would soon come to an end. The more they advanced however, the more devastation and misery the troops saw that the enemy had inflicted on their own people. On May 8 1945, the war in Europe eventually came to an end, and David was thankful that he and most of his men had survived, but shed a tear for his parents.

Within days of the victory, David, along with many others, was sent further east. When they reached their destination they were escorted to a huge military type camp; the men who had run the camp had either fled the area or had been taken prisoner and shot, when the allies advanced. What they saw was an unbelievable scene of human cruelty: there were hundreds, if not thousands of emaciated people walking around, and many more, too weak to walk were lying on the ground. Mounds of rotting corpses were everywhere, and a smell of death lingered over the camp. For some of the poor souls there was nothing that could be done and they soon faded away. For those that could be helped it was a slow process; food had to be provided and the poor people needed to be cleaned, sanitised and sprayed with powder to delouse them.

As David was passing a soldier spraying the survivors with powder, he noticed a woman in the queue; what a pitiful sight she presented with her loose fitting dress, tufts of hair sticking out of her shaven head, sunken eyes and a bag of bones for a body. In her arms she clutched a bundle of rags to her chest, you could not say breasts, for the poor soul seemed not to have any. David thought that the bundle was probably an infant, as she wouldn't part with. The soldier spraying them wasn't taking the job seriously and was laughing. When it was the turn of the woman to be deloused, the soldier was laughing as he sprayed her underneath her dress.

'Haven't these poor souls suffered enough with out you adding to it?' shouted David. 'Show some compassion man, or I'll have you on a charge of misconduct of duty, and I'll see to it that the charge sticks.'

'Yes sergeant,' answered the soldier.

At that moment David was called away, and it was not until later when he was sat on his own that his thoughts returned to incident that he had witnessed. The way the woman was holding the bundle of rags to her chest seemed to haunt him. Try as he could he could not pinpoint why it should be so vivid in his mind. Then it came to him, the way the woman had held the bundle was so like the way Rosa had held her violin case, when he rescued her from the dog. Surely the poor soul he had seen earlier in the day could not be Rosa. If she was still alive could that really be her here in this camp?

The next day he could not get to the office quick enough to find out this person's whereabouts. To his dismay he learnt that she had been shipped out of the camp soon after she had been sprayed. She was only one of many displaced persons without identification who were being transported to Russia.

David tried so hard to try and find out who this woman was, but it was a difficult task as most of the records had been destroyed before the camp had been liberated. He just wanted some confirmation that this was Rosa, even though deep down he was convinced that the woman who had stood in front of him was the same woman who had stood before him in that red dress and played her violin all those years before.

Meanwhile Rosa was on a train heading miles away from David and the camp. The train's conditions were not the best, but much better than when she had travelled from France to the camp; at least she now had a seat, clean clothes and as much food as she could eat, which was not much. Most of all she still had her violin with her, even if it was wrapped in a bundle of old rags.

The people in charge of the train were all military personnel and so everything was very strict, but kindness was shown to her and the other survivors from the camp - anything was better than what she had experienced. When they eventually reached their destination, it was again a military camp where they were to be housed for the time being. Food, shelter and clothes were provided, and they began to grow stronger and fitter with time.

As each day dawned her body and mind grew a little stronger and life began to take on a new, more positive meaning. Before her were clear blue skies and fresh air: the smell of the camp was behind her now forever, or so she hoped.

Rosa shared the hut she now lived in, with Abe and Maria, a couple, who like her had managed to survive the camp. They were middle-aged, good people who had lost all their family in the camp and now regarded Rosa as their own. Rosa, too, began to look upon them as parents.

Autumn passed to winter, and then spring came, and Abe and Maria were told that they were to be given accommodation outside the camp. As there was enough room, they asked Rosa if she would like to move in with them. She agreed and soon joined them; this new 'family' enjoyed returning to a normal life after the years in the camp.

One day, Rosa came home very excited, and said she had heard that some people could emigrate to Israel if they wished and should she put their names down? After a lot of discussion, they agreed that all three should apply immediately. After stringent medicals that they all passed, their names were put on the list to leave for Israel in the near future.

Eventually the day arrived when the three of them were to pack, which did not take long as they had so few possessions, except a few clothes, and of course, Rosa's violin. The journey took many days travelling by train and then ship, which was crowded with immigrants from the camps. To the passengers it seemed like a pleasure cruise as they were journeying to freedom and the hope of starting a new and better life in the "promised land".

CHAPTER 13

ROSA, ABE AND MARIA, who she now regarded as her adopted parents, along with many more of the ship's passengers were placed in a kibbutz in the country, not far from the port where they had arrived. Being in Israel was a new start for all of them. There was marvellous sunshine, good food and fresh fruit for the picking, and the freedom and peace of mind did wonders for all of them.

They were all given paid work. The kibbutz was self-sufficient, they lived off of the land and their animals and any surplus was sold and the profits shared equally among the group.

Being near the sea meant that it was ideal for any leisure time which Rosa and her younger friends enjoyed; playing carefree on a beach helped her life to return to something like normality and to forget the horrors of the camp. A marvellous transformation had taken place in her appearance: her dark hair had grown back to its normal long length, her figure had filled out again, and she now seemed more like the pre-war Rosa.

In the kibbutz they had many forms of entertainment for off duty hours. A small orchestra had been formed, and Rosa played in it when she was available. It was a long time since Rosa had felt so happy, alive, content and most of all free. Sometimes when she was alone, her mind drifted back to the happy memories of her childhood in England. Then thoughts of the camps: the beatings and those terrible conditions, which almost deprived her of life invaded her thoughts, but being Rosa, she tried to put these out of her mind and get on with her new life, and be thankful that she had survived.

Since her release from the concentration camp Rosa had tried many times to contact her parents in England. She had had little success while she was living in Russia, and she hoped that it would be easier to contact them from Israel. She knew that they had left their hometown, but no one seemed to know where they had gone. She thought they might have gone to live in the country to escape the bombing, which had been heavy at times and had destroyed several parts of the town. She longed to know whether they were still alive.

One day when Rosa was playing a solo with the kibbutz orchestra, an eminent musician who was visiting the kibbutz heard her, and asked if he could be introduced to her. Later that evening they met, he asked her about her music background, where she had studied and who her tutor had been. When she told him her story, and how she had survived the camp, he could hardly believe what he was hearing. When she told him who her tutor had been in France, he said, 'I am not surprised you are so good, you studied with one of the world's greatest violinists. He did not waste his time in teaching you, and if you continue to play as I have heard you play today, his memory will live on. You are a superb player, and I think you will improve with every performance. I will make enquiries for you to have an audition with the Israeli National Orchestra, if you wish?'

Rosa could hardly believe what she had just heard, and could not get back quick enough to tell Abe and Maria her good news. It was hard to tell which of the three of them was most pleased with the news, for they were all so excited and proud.

The musician kept his word, and in due course Rosa was invited to go for an audition with the National Orchestra. When she arrived at the hall where rehearsals were taking place, she felt a little nervous; the size of the auditorium and the number of musicians amazed her. The conductor of the orchestra was not the man who had spoken to her in the kibbutz, but when she was introduced to him he made her feel most welcome and tried to allay her fears. He asked her if she would play lead violinist, and when that piece was finished if she would then play solo with the full orchestra. After both pieces the whole orchestra rose to a standing ovation with continued applause. The conductor was more than pleased with her performance and said that he was sure that he could find her a place in the orchestra. He knew that with more practice, and with the full orchestra she could become one of the finest solo artists in the world.

By now Rosa had taken her St Christopher medallion from the inside of her violin, where she had hidden it, and placed it around her neck once more. When she was asked about it, she said her parents had given it to her, and along with her violin, it was her most treasured possession in the world. She explained that the medallion was one of a pair that had been given at the same time: one to her and one to a very dear friend whom she doubted she would ever see again. David like so many important people in her life had disappeared, and she didn't know whether she would see them again.

Abe and Maria had not been at the audition as work at the kibbutz took priority, but when Rosa arrived home she told them about her performance and the standing ovation, and they were overjoyed. They thought that she was a good musician after hearing her practice, but did not realise how good she was. That night the topic of conversation was about music and the National Orchestra. Not having played in a professional orchestra before, Rosa knew that if she was asked to join she would have to practice a lot, and commit her future life to her music. She told Abe and Maria that if she was accepted, they too would be part of her new life, for it would be different to what they now had in the kibbutz: it would mean more money and a different lifestyle, and she wanted to share it with them. Wherever she went in the future, she wanted them to accompany her: be it good or bad, they were so much a part of her life now as the breath that she breathed.

Confirmation soon came to say that she had been accepted to join the orchestra on a trial period. She could hardly wait, and very soon she became part of the musical world in Israel. She was an easy person to get on with, and everyone soon welcomed and accepted her. She loved every minute of her newfound lifestyle, and found that the more she played the better she became; whether she was playing or practising. She never seemed to tire and enjoyed every minute. The orchestra was soon to go on a tour that would take Rosa away from home for a while. Abe and Maria said that they would not go along with her, for there was a lot of work to do at home. When the time came for Rosa to leave them she was so tearful at the parting, that she upset them too. As soon as she reached her destination she was on the phone to them, and throughout the tour kept in touch with them at least twice a day. She decided then that if the orchestra was not performing too far from home that Abe and Maria would accompany her. Half way through the tour, the lead violinist had an accident, and Rosa was asked to replace him, which she did with great success.

Life for Rosa had taken on a new meaning for her now that she was with the orchestra. It was surprising how time passed, and she decided to enjoy her new lifestyle and put her terrible past behind her and look only to the future.

* * * * *

When David finished work at the concentration camp where Rosa had been, he was sent to the army of occupation until demobilisation in the late spring of 1946. He did not return to England straightaway but decided to try and find Rosa; such was his conviction that it had been her that he had seen many months ago being sprayed with powder. He wore his uniform, which meant that it was easier to go from country to country in his search for her. Unfortunately he soon found that it was like looking for a needle in a haystack, as he had no photo of her and soon realised that he was having no success and decided to admit defeat and return home to England.

He had received news that both his brothers had survived the war and were well. William was back in London at his old pre-war job and was now married to Kathleen. Alfred had survived the horrors of a Japanese prisoner of war camp, and had decided that he would make a new life for himself in the Far East.

Once back in England, David found he had no job, no home and very little money. He decided to visit William, whom he had not seen since before their parents' death. Both William and Kathleen made David feel very welcome, and he was more than pleased for somewhere to stay. However, he did not wish to impose himself on to them for too long, and so was constantly on the lookout for opportunities to earn some money.

As he travelled through London, he noticed the amount of rubble and war damage still lying about, on what people called "bombsites". His business mind started working, and he began to formulate a plan to make money, all he needed was some capital to get him started.

One morning whilst he was waiting at a bus stop in the city, he noticed a man walking by. The man was tall, erect with a good bearing; he wore a dark suit, a bowler hat and carried a brief case. David immediately recognised the man, and decided to follow him. Eventually the man reached a large building and entered, David did not follow but took notice of the address and went on his way.

During the next few days, David made many enquiries regarding his business proposal. When he had acquired the information he needed, and made the relevant calculations, he gave a smile of satisfaction.

The next day he made himself very presentable and proceeded to the large building that was a merchant bank. The name on the plaque confirmed to him that the man who he had seen was who he thought he was, and David entered, determined to see him.

Once inside, he enquired if he could see the person in question. He was told 'No', in a most official manner by the secretary. David didn't move, and again asked very politely if he could see the man in question.

'No,' came the answer from the secretary, 'he does not

see anyone without an appointment and that could take some time. I'm his private secretary, and his diary is very full.' Once again David didn't move. He asked if the man in question was in his office and if so, would she be kind enough to say just one word: "serpent". He told her that he would wait here until she returned, and then if there were no answer, he would go and never return.

The secretary knocked on the door entered and said, 'Please sir, I have a young man in the office who is most intent on seeing you, shall I tell him to go? He didn't give a name, but told me to say just one word "serpent".'

'Please show him straight in,' came the reply.

She turned, went through the door and told the young man he could go into the room. As David entered, the man was rising from his chair behind a huge desk and shook David firmly by the hand.

'Cancel all the appointments I have today except the one at 3.30pm, which I must attend to,' said the man to the secretary.

'But sir you have so many appointments booked for today,' came the reply.

'I said cancel them, do you understand?'

She knew by the tone of his voice that she had better do as he said. Straightaway David knew that he had been right when he saw the man in the street a few days ago; it was his old Commanding Officer, the one who first trained him, and who went with him on the raid to the weather station.

'Sit down Jones. It is Jones isn't it?' he asked. 'To me you will always be Jones, don't like first names, can't get used to them.'

'Well to me you will always be Sir,' answered David.

'Now tell me all about your service days and adventures, most of which I missed, not through choice I can tell you. After the first raid you and I went on, they moved me to be a desk soldier. Somehow I got promotion, though why I don't know, and I ended up as a Colonel. I helped with the planning of D Day, but they wouldn't let me fight, left that to such chaps as you I guess, and you all did such a good job, I'm pleased to say.'

After a while, the Colonel called his secretary and asked for coffee. When she brought it in, the Colonel asked David if he was free for lunch. David said that he was free all day, and so the Colonel instructed his secretary to book lunch at his gentleman's club.

'Tell them that I have a very special guest, and that we would like good portions of fish and poultry. Can't wait until this damned rationing is finished, and we can have plenty of good meat again, I'm sick of fish and poultry.'

The Colonel asked David many questions about his service life, which left David no time to say why he had paid the Colonel a visit in the first place. However, just before lunch, David did manage to say that he was here on business and that he would like to discuss a business proposal.

The Colonel signed David into his club, and asked him if he would have a drink, which David declined. The Colonel ordered his usual drink of whisky and soda. The club was magnificent in every respect: the decoration, the furniture and the carpets. The building itself had been lucky not to have been damaged by bombs during the war. As usual it was well patronised, the Colonel acknowledged one or two with his customary nod, and then took David to a corner of the room, which was more private.

David gave the Colonel a quick account of his life before he joined the Army; about the cart he had as a boy, the shipyard and then his cycle venture and his own shop. The Colonel was most impressed by what David had told him, by then they were told that lunch was being served, and they moved into the restaurant. The meal was taken in semi silence, as David knew enough about etiquette not to speak of business during lunch. The fish and poultry were excellent, and David lost no time in saying so and thanked the Colonel for his hospitality. They left the table to take coffee in the corner where they had previously sat. It was then that David outlined his business plan, and hoped that he had not wasted the Colonel's time.

'Indeed you have not my boy, I think you have some excellent ideas, and I'm sure that you and I can put some of them into practice.'

The two had not gone unnoticed in the club, and quite a few members said to one another, 'I wonder what the colonel has in mind? The wily old fox will have something in his future plans. As for the young chap he seems to be a stranger and I wonder where he'll fit in.'

Time seemed to pass so quickly, and the Colonel asked if he could be excused, as he had a very important meeting later that afternoon. He asked if he could have David's address in case he needed to contact him. He also asked David if he could be in his office in a week's time with details of locations, equipment and prices relating to his business proposal. David gave William's address, and thought about all the work that he would have to do before their next meeting. He said goodbye to the Colonel and they both went their separate ways.

When next week came, David had not wasted his time and had obtained the information that the Colonel had wanted and more for their next meeting. David received a letter from the Colonel's secretary, confirming the date and time of the meeting. David was on time, and this time was shown straight into the Colonel's office, he then set about presenting his business plan.

London and many other cities had suffered bomb damage, and it was the removal of the rubble that interested David. He said that most of the work would have to be done by private enterprise, and the sooner the sites were cleared the better. Equipment was not too readily available for such work, however army surplus war material such as ex-Army vehicles, bulldozers, road rollers, and construction materials together with spare parts for repair and maintenance were now surplus to requirements and were to be sold by auction in the near future; a large part of all this material would end up as scrap metal. One could not do much clearance with one three ton ex-Army lorry, but 50 to 60 such vehicles could soon make a difference in days, not weeks once the vehicles had been modified, canvas tops removed. Once the sites were cleared of their rubble and the craters filled in, expensive building land would be revealed.

The more that David described his ideas to him, the more the Colonel became interested. Here was a young man who was very ambitious and had an eye for the future. Here was a young man who was very similar to what he had been at David's age, and maybe between them they could help each other, to rebuild a new London and maybe other parts of England too.

By the time the discussion came to a close, it was difficult to choose which of the two was the most interested party in the proposed project. The Colonel said he would put the proposal to his board to seek approval, and make enquiries both financial and legal, and that he would let David know their decision in the near future. There was a lot of money and risk involved, and he told David not to be disappointed if nothing came of his ideas. He told him not to give up hope if he did not get the approval of the board, as he was sure that something would turn up for David in the future.

That evening when the Colonel and his wife were having dinner, he mentioned David to her for the first time. He told her how David had served under him in the Army, how he had worked as a youngster while still at school, about his shop, and about the loss of his parents. When he had finished, she seemed to show nearly as much interest as the Colonel, and asked him to keep her informed of any future progress with the venture.

When the bank board next met, the Colonel brought David's idea forward. He did not disclose his past background or much about him, deciding to concentrate more on the proposal in hand. He must have done David justice because the proposal was passed unanimously. Each member of the board realised that it was a huge project, and that a lot of finance would be involved, but they could also see that the reward for success was enormous.

David was asked to a meeting with the Colonel again very soon, and many things were discussed: which site was to be cleared first, where to put the debris, which ex-military vehicles and equipment were to be purchased, at what price and by whom, where to place the site office and how many drivers and maintenance mechanics would be needed? David suggested it should be run like a military operation. He had also found out where and when the sale of some of ex-military equipment was to be held. He had also found out the address of one of his former service pals who was a marvellous mechanic, and together they agreed to go and check out the vehicles and other equipment before the sale. The vehicles and equipment at the sale were all in very good condition. David was armed with a banker's draft, and was able to purchase most of his requirements at a very reasonable price, along with many spare parts for future repairs.

Before work started David painted all the vehicles bright red, to cover the Army camouflage, together with a motif of his old pre-war cart. This was to become his trademark and would be easily recognisable for years to come. When all the formalities were in place, work began on removing the debris, with a lot of the responsibility falling on David.

When the board first sanctioned the loan, the Colonel had formed a company. David put what little money he had into the company, and the Colonel, unbeknown to his wife, put some of his money into the company for her, because of her interest in David's venture.

The enthusiasm that David showed rubbed off on to his workmen. Soon the money started to come in and the company began to grow swiftly. Site after site was cleared; the cost for clearing a site was not cheap, particularly if it could not be purchased. The loan for the equipment was soon paid off; there was still much work to do and David's bank balance was growing.

David found alternative living accommodation, because he did not think it was right to impose on William and Kathleen's hospitality any longer than was necessary. They had been so very kind when it was needed and he would not forget it in the future.

David and the Colonel were very much in touch business wise, and if David ever had a problem he always consulted his partner, which the Colonel appreciated. When a site was for sale after clearance, it was bought and used as a car park until planning permission and building materials became available and it could be developed.

It was surprising how the time seemed to fly, days turned to weeks and weeks to months. Although he was so busy he never forgot to visit William and Kathleen and when he could, he would take them out for a meal. They all got on so well together.

As things progressed, David had quite a work force to manage. He delegated work to those whom he thought could achieve the best results and so far his judgement had not been wrong. Now they were in the building trade, quite a lot of responsibility fell on to his shoulders which he seemed to relish; he had to attend planning committees, meet with architects and builders, and it was surprising how quickly David became an adept businessman. The more work that came his way the more he seemed to cope. Now that he was in a supervisory capacity, he had his own office and like the Colonel his own secretary. The cart logo on the vehicles was now on all the business paper and was becoming easily recognisable in London, even William had noticed it many times and mentioned it to David when they next met.

Many buildings were constructed: many offices, some shops; then planning permission was granted for one large sight that had been earmarked for a hotel, and work commenced, as it did with many more projects. David often remarked that it was a good job that he was not married and had no current lady friend, as his work took up such a lot of his time.

A couple of years had passed since David had first met with the Colonel. The hotel, which was in a prominent area of London, was nearing completion; it had been a huge project, with many construction problems, but these had been solved. It was a very attractive building and, although modern, was in keeping with the surrounding buildings.

One weekend David was invited to a shooting party at the Colonel's home in the country. There were spare sporting guns so he need not go and purchase any. The Colonel laughed as he said, 'I know you have Wellington boots, I have seen you wear them. I have seen you busy on sites quite a few times, when you have not seen me.' When David said he would be delighted to accept the invitation, the Colonel seemed very pleased.

David drove down to the Tate's in his car. Their home was a country estate in a very beautiful part of England; the house was not too large, but not tiny by any means. When David drove down the drive, it reminded him of his childhood, when he had walked back up the drive at the big house after delivering the lady's cycle and had seen people dancing for the first time. He remembered asking his Mum to teach him to dance, and how they had both enjoyed themselves many years ago. But that seemed like a lifetime away, and so much had changed in his life since then. He slowed the car almost to a walking pace so he could keep these memories in his mind's eye for a little longer.

CHAPTER 14

DAVID PULLED UP and looked at the front of the house. He got out of the car, opened the boot and took out his case. He rang the doorbell and waited until a young maid opened the door. He told her his name, and she asked him to step inside as Colonel Tate was expecting him. The Colonel appeared, shook David by the hand, inquired about his journey and introduced him to Mrs Tate.

Mrs Tate, or Laura as she was called, was more or less as David had imagined her to be: a medium built middle-aged woman, with a delicate complexion, who was softly spoken and very pleasant. She soon made David feel very welcome and quickly put him at his ease. The maid returned from taking David's case upstairs, and then showed him to his room that was en-suite, and like the rest of the house had a nice décor.

David had arrived before the other guests; Mrs Tate said that there was no hurry and that he could take his time unpacking. When David did come down, the Colonel was waiting in the lounge for him and asked if he would like a drink, which he accepted. As there was only the two of them in the room, they were able to talk freely to each other, and the Colonel said that the shooting party was mostly to be made up of politicians. He advised David not to try and prove himself as a marksman, even though he knew that he was a good shot from his experience in the war. He told him that it paid dividends to let the politicians think that they were good at the sport.

'Let them think that they hold sway, even though we know that it is men like us in grey suits, who are the real masters. Whatever colour the politicians are, red, blue or yellow they are the government for only a short time, it is the men in grey who are there forever. And now, Jones, you are a man in grey like me, and it is us who have the power. Keep a low profile, look, listen and learn. Being a Yorkshire man, it should be easy for you to listen and say nothing.'

David thanked the Colonel for his drink and said he would do his best to follow his instructions at the shoot, and to heed his advice in the future. By now some of the other guests had started to arrive. David asked if he might take a walk around the grounds prior to dinner, and so excused himself and went outside. The weather was pleasant and so he walked at a leisurely pace through the grounds, he looked at the avenue of trees which were still in leaf, the sky, the beds of flowers and the well kept lawns, and he seemed more at ease than he had done in a long time. Work on all the projects was on schedule and going to plan, which was a change, but he knew this would only be temporary. It was nice to get away from the pressures of work for a few days, and he enjoyed the relaxing walk. A couple of squirrels were busy running up and down the trees, their bushy tails sticking up; the birds were singing and flying from tree to tree, and just for a moment his thoughts went back to his Father's allotment when he was a boy, which now seemed so far away. It was surprising how long he had spent in the grounds enjoying the tranquillity and being in touch with nature. Looking at his watch, he was surprised at the time, and realised that he should be getting ready for dinner. He quickly made his way indoors, bathed and dressed in his dinner jacket, as this was a very formal weekend and went downstairs.

During the cocktails, Mrs Tate introduced David to the guests, and then it was time for the meal. Mrs Tate had made a good table plan, sitting alternate male and female where she could. She sat David next to herself and then on his other side was a lady who Mrs Tate knew would put him at his ease, and who would not be too inquisitive; such was her thoughtfulness. The meal took a long time, everyone agreed that the food was excellent, and David felt comfortable in the company of these people. Mrs Tate was a perfect hostess in every way, as a stranger, she had made David feel completely at ease throughout the entire evening.

At one part of the conversation during the meal, the subject turned to vacations, and how more people were taking their holidays abroad. The lady on David's left said she and her husband had been to Israel a short while ago, partly on business but taking a few days out as a holiday, and whilst they were there, they had been invited to a concert by the state orchestra. They had been very impressed by one of the violinists who was leaving to start on a world tour as a solo artist. She did not say if it was a male or female musician, and the topic of conversation soon changed. At the end of the evening before retiring, David thanked Mrs Tate for a lovely evening, saying that it was a long time since he had enjoyed himself so much.

The next day the shoot went off marvellously. David did as he had been instructed, and did not shoot too well, which more than pleased the Colonel. He watched the Colonel and realised what a smooth operator he was, and that he was teaching David lessons that would benefit him in the future.

Before David departed for home, he managed a quick chat with the Colonel. He asked him whether he thought Mrs Tate would be interested in joining the team of interior designers in the decoration of the hotel. He hoped the Colonel did not mind him asking, but after seeing how tastefully decorated their home was, he thought that she was ideal to help with choosing colours, carpets and furniture, and of course, she was a share holder in the company, so who better? The Colonel thanked David, and said that he would ask if she was interested, and would let David know in the near future.

When all their guests had departed and they were alone, the Colonel thanked his wife for being such a marvellous hostess in helping make the weekend such a success. He then put David's proposal to her, and asked her if she would be interested in designing the interior of the new hotel.

'Is this in payment for giving you a good weekend's shoot?' she asked laughing. 'What woman would not like such a challenge? It is what most women dream of doing, spending lots of money and knowing that their husband is not going to scold them for it. Is this a gift from you? I thank you with all of my heart my darling.'

'Actually it was David's idea not mine. So if you do accept, drop him a line and thank him personally. Now come and give me a kiss.'

As she sat with her arm around him, she said, 'It is the first time I have met David, and I was very impressed with him, and I know you like him. He once served under your command, didn't he?

'He did, and even then I could see that he had what it takes.'

'I was just wondering,' said Mrs Tate, 'is there a lady in his life? He didn't bring a wife or lady friend with him this weekend, and he is very attractive.'

'Now my dear,' he laughed, 'you're a true woman, wondering what he gets up to, and what secrets he holds. Anyway he can't have you so there, and I'll have another kiss before you get me another drink,' and he patted her bottom as she got up and passed him.

But Laura was not the only one who had such doubts. The Colonel had been in David's company many times now, and the females had never been discussed even though he had spoken of Laura in the past quite a few times to him.

Within a few days Mrs Tate wrote David a handwritten letter thanking him for asking her to oversee the interior design of the new hotel, and said that she was looking forward to working with him. She hoped that he could manage a little time from his already busy life to sit in with the designers and her, and give his final approval to any ideas that she presented.

Work on all fronts seemed to go very well; more sites were purchased and office blocks, for which there was a market demand, were built once materials and labour became available. It was surprising how much revenue they accumulated with these and other business ventures the company had entered into.

One day when they were holding a business meeting with their lawyer and accountant, David announced that when the hotel was finished he might decide to live there if he could afford it. The accountant smiled and said, 'Afford it, you could own it if you wished, never mind rent a room.'

Mrs Tate and the interior decorators had done a marvellous job, no expense was spared; the hotel was now a quality building both inside and out, and was a credit to all who had worked on the project. The most splendid room was the ballroom: the chandeliers hung over a huge dance floor, which was sprung making it a pleasure to dance on. David hoped that he would be able to use it one day, but as of yet he had no idea who his partner would be. The first time he saw the ballroom completed he thought how he would like to have danced with his mother in a setting like this; and how pleased she would be to think that he had achieved so much. He became sad when he thought that he seemed to have acquired so much of late, and yet seemed to have so little. However he was looking forward to living in the hotel, now that it was almost ready for guests.

Although it was expensive, the hotel was very busy as it was in central London, and David thought that they had made a good move building it there. As he was living there, he could keep an eye on the day to day running of the hotel, and this kept the staff on their toes. He wasn't a nuisance, but nothing escaped him from the quality of the food to the room service, which helped maintain a high standard.

This made the Colonel laugh, 'Can't forget your days as an NCO can you Jones? And not a bad thing either, since we started our venture, it has paid dividends you being in command and being there on the job when it was required.'

'Must have been a good tutor,' said Jones giving the Colonel a wink, 'and one that none of us dared disobey.'

'Can you spare the time for a drink?' asked David.

'If I can't I'll make time,' said the Colonel.

Many things were quickly discussed over the drink and David asked to be remembered to Mrs Tate. He never called her Laura to the Colonel, or anyone else for that matter, not even when they worked together during the hotel project. He said what a good job Mrs Tate had done, and that many of her ideas had been accepted without question by the design team. In return for all her hard work, David invited them to accompany him to the theatre and to stay at the hotel as his guests.

Before they left, David informed the Colonel that he had one or two more projects in the pipeline, and would keep him informed if and when anything materialised. Things were moving at a fast pace, and they had to be one step ahead of their competitors. They finished their drinks, shook hands as they said goodbye, and went their separate ways.

David had never forgotten the kindness that Mrs Thomas, his mother's old friend, had shown him when he had nowhere to stay after his home had been bombed. He had kept in touch with her ever since, writing to her a couple of times and always sending a Christmas card and a small present. Much as he would have liked to correspond with Nancy, he had never done so, just the annual Christmas card that was always very formal. But both Nancy and Rosa were never far from his mind when he was in a pensive mood. He came into contact with many women his own age and younger, yet none had seemed to come up to his expectations, or seemed to have what he wanted. Some he had even spent the night with in discreet surroundings. So unlike his older brother, who although not rich was happy with his wife and young family, he had not met and married a woman he loved. Once again his thoughts went back to when he was a child, and to when he watched his Mum sort out the meagre amounts of money in the days of the strike. He could hear her say that, "Money was the root of all evils, but I would not mind a few more roots this week, and I would not try and do evil things with them." Such thoughts went as soon as they came, which is as well, for one cannot live in the past, but yet one can never forget such memories.

One day David's secretary gave him a letter as he entered the office, she knew it was personal so had not opened it. It bore a New Zealand stamp, and was from his old army friend Paul. After the war he had emigrated to New Zealand and had made a new life there. The letter said that he was returning to England to marry one of his old girlfriends, and that he would honeymoon in England and then return to New Zealand. Paul was asked if David would do him the honour of being his best man. He had obtained David's address from his Christmas cards to Nancy. The thought of seeing Nancy again excited him beyond belief, and must have shown in his face as his secretary said, 'Good news sir?'

'You could say that,' he answered as he folded the letter and put it in his pocket, and then continued with the business of the day. When alone, he read the letter again: Paul wrote that because the bride's mother had been ill, much of the preparation had fallen on Nancy's shoulders, and she had arranged that the wedding party would go from her home, and for those who had to stay the night, hotel accommodation could be booked. David quickly wrote an answer to Paul, saying that he would be delighted to be his best man and wished him all the luck for the future.

The wedding was to be a formal occasion, so he was measured for his suit, and had it delivered well before the day. David wondered if Nancy had changed much, and how she would receive him when they met. Both she and Rosa had seemed to play such an important part in his life, and yet he had spent so little time with either of them.

On the day of the wedding he set off early, and arrived in good time at Nancy's home. He parked his car, opened the boot and took out his case, for he expected that he and the bridegroom would be leaving from Nancy's home. He rang the doorbell, and after a short pause, the door was opened by a young lady, who David recognised from her photograph, as Nancy's daughter. Both gave a smile, and David said, 'I'm David, I think I'm expected.'

'Please come in. I'm Gail, I'm pleased to meet you,' she said, shaking David's hand now he had put down the case. 'Mum and Daddy are busy just at present, so may I show you to your room?' As they walked up the stairs to his room, she said, 'Uncle Paul will be along later, and since it is quite a while since you last met, no doubt you will have a lot to talk about, and not too much time in which to reminisce, pity you could not have met up sooner.' When they got to the door she said, 'Please don't be too long as I know both Mum and Daddy are anxious to meet you, see you later then.'

When David left his room and went downstairs, Nancy and Ted were waiting to greet him. The years had been good to Nancy, for she had changed little since he last saw her. Nancy shook him by the hand, then half turning said, 'This is my husband Edward, or Ted, as he likes to be called. You have never met previously, but I told Ted about how you and Paul spent a few days here on leave just before you went to France. Would you like some tea or coffee?'

'Coffee would be very nice, please,' answered David.

Nancy left to get the coffee, and David and Ted exchanged polite conversation about his journey and the wedding plans until Nancy, joined by Gail, returned with the coffee.

A little later in the morning Ted said to Gail, 'I have met David before, but I can't think where, or when, but I will remember and I hope it comes back to me soon.'

Ted soon remembered where he had seen David before, and he asked him, 'Weren't you the NCO who was wounded with about six or more other chaps, one really shot up, and you pleaded, almost begged me not to amputate his arm?'

'Yes I was that NCO, sir' said David, 'although I never saw your face because you wore a gauze mask which hid your face.'

'Well I guess that soldier should thank you for his arm as well as me, probably more you, David, as I was about to cut it off until you requested that I try and save it, which I did. Mind you, I missed a pork dinner doing it though.'

'No more sirs please,' said Ted, 'now I am Ted, not sir, we are not in the army anymore.'

Ted had returned from the war back to his old job at the hospital. He had written a paper on the operation he had performed on the soldier's arm years ago, which was published in medical journals, and was helping to advance surgery in many areas. As a result he was highly respected in the medical profession, but was content to live his life as it had been in pre-war days.

A little later he told Gail that he had remembered where he and David had met, and under what circumstances. Ted said that when he was a boy his parents had an old spaniel dog, and if it was ever scolded it looked back at them with such beautiful wide eyes so that it always got a pat on the head to remove the appealing look. It was a similar appealing look that David had given him when he tried to save that arm. He told her how David had been in great pain from his own wounds, but had insisted that all his men should be attended to first, such was the calibre of the man.

'So both you and Mum had met David before?' said Gail.

'Yes, but under different circumstances,' said Ted. 'I recognised him, but he didn't me because of the mask that I was wearing at the time. It has been so nice meeting up with him again after so long. In those days he looked like a mere boy, but nowadays he looks older, more mature and no doubt he is.'

After a few minutes had passed someone asked who was to collect the flowers from the florist. David offered to go, if someone could direct him there. It was almost time for Paul to be picked up from the station so they could also collect him at the same time. Nancy volunteered to direct, and so in next to no time they were in David's car and on their way. Before they reached the end of the drive they were asking each other questions, catching up on what each had done since they had last met. Both said that they thought they would never see each other again, and were delighted that this opportunity to meet again had come. The journey to the florists and the station did not take long, but as the train was late it gave them more time to talk, as they sat on the platform. It was not long before both said how they had enjoyed the last time they had met, and how often each had reminisced about those few days. As they were sat there, Nancy placed her hand in his and gave it a little squeeze.

'Is there a Mrs Jones, or a special lady friend in your life David?' she asked. 'Or should I not ask?'

'Since my Mum was killed, there are just two now.' He did not say too much, only that one was a Jewess, and he did not think anything would come of it, as he was not sure where in the world she was. The other was a married lady, who he would never try and take away from her family as he knew that she loved and cared for them very much. He was also indebted to her husband, as he had granted him a favour a few years ago that he would never forget. With that Paul's train arrived at the station. She gave his hand an extra squeeze before releasing his grip and smiled, for she knew who the latter person was, and it was hard for her to keep back a tear. Paul was soon on the platform, hugging and kissing Nancy, and shaking David warmly by the hand.

They were soon back at the house where they had a drink and a light snack, and then it was time for the wedding, which thanks to Nancy's preparations went very well. David thought that both Nancy and Gail looked very beautiful, as did everyone else, but it was Nancy he most admired.

Later when Gail and her father were talking, she said to him that she had noticed David looking at Nancy whilst the speeches were being given. She had seen the look in David's eyes that her father had described in the Spaniel's eyes: a look of hurt, of wanting, and of real love. She wondered who David was thinking about, probably a woman who was not present at that moment in time.

Later that evening, David asked Nancy for a dance, which they both enjoyed. He danced with the bride, with Gail and one or two more of the female guests. When the time came for him to leave and return to London, he needed to change and pick up his luggage from Ted and Nancy's. Nancy said that if he would take her back to the dance then she would go with him to the house. He agreed, said his goodbyes to all, and he and Nancy were soon away. David soon changed, packed, and was downstairs where Nancy was waiting for him, before they locked the door David thanked Nancy and said how much he had enjoyed the day, and meeting Ted and Gail, and of course her again. Nancy said that she remembered the last dance they were at, and when they arrived back home how David had asked if he may kiss her, this time it was she who asked him for a kiss.

'I have been wanting to hold and kiss you ever since we met this morning,' said David, and with that they were in each other's arms.

'When I kiss you,' said Nancy, 'I feel sixteen again, just like I felt when we danced the night away during the war. When we had that dance tonight I did not want it to end, and I was jealous of those that you danced with later, even Gail, which I know is wrong and I thank you for being David, my David, please don't ever change.'

When they were in the car going back to the dance, he asked if she would grant him one request, she said if it was possible, she would. He said that there were three hundred and sixty five days in a year and please could he have just one day; for three hundred and sixty four days her husband could have her, but for that day he wanted her to himself and no one else. They could meet in London, on a day just before Christmas so that she could be his special Christmas present, the one he wanted the most from Father Christmas. They could spend the whole day together and at the end of the visit he would send her back to Ted, as he had so much respect for them both. If she could not accept the offer, he would understand and never think any the less of her. She laughed and said, 'Of course I will. Aren't I lucky to be loved by two marvellous men? David you know I would never hurt either or you.'

The car seemed to take them back to the dance quicker than either of them wanted. Nancy just gave his hand a squeeze in case anyone was watching her alight from the car, then said, ' 'Til Christmas, my David, now go and find your Jewess and I wish you all the luck in the world.'

Once Nancy had got out of the car, it seemed a long journey back to his hotel and he did not rush. He had seen Nancy again, she had not changed too much in her appearance, but best of all she was still the person he loved and hopefully he would spend a day with her before Christmas.

When Nancy, Ted and Gail were having an evening meal soon after the wedding, the topic of conversation somehow centred on David. Gail said that she was surprised that he was not married, or at least he had not brought a lady with him to the wedding. He had a nice car and seemed well provided for, but never disclosed what line of business he was in, discussed his lifestyle or his family. He was very handsome and a good dancer, and all in all seemed a very nice young man. Nancy said she knew that his parents had been killed in an air raid, and until the wedding had not seen him since the few days leave he and Paul spent with her, which seemed ages ago now. Paul had told her a long time ago that he was a quiet sort of person who kept himself to himself and did not seek the company of females. Nancy said she had heard from somewhere that two women had played a large part in his life: one was a Jewess and the other a married woman, and as he could never have either he was a very unhappy, disappointed young man. However her impression of him was of a very kind and considerate man and a person who would never try to hurt anyone or come between man and wife. Once she had said it, she had a silent thought to herself, although she was a good wife to Ted in everyway she would never hurt him intentionally or betray him, but when David held and kissed her she felt a different person, and knew if it was possible she would spend that one day with him prior to Christmas. After all, Ted did have her for three hundred and sixty four days a year as David had said, and although it was possible that both she and David probably desired each other, she knew that neither would yield to temptation. To be loved and kissed by him was enough for her, and she hoped it would be the same for him too.

CHAPTER 15

SINCE BEING IN ISRAEL, Rosa was a changed person; whether it was the warm sunshine, the food, the freedom, the happy existence or maybe a culmination of them all, she looked and felt fine. Abe and Maria were also well, and the three of them made a happy trio. They certainly took care of Rosa and she them.

The orchestra was sorry to lose Rosa, who was about to embark on a solo world tour. She too, was sorry to be leaving them and Israel, but her future prospects were too good an opportunity to turn down, especially as this was something that she had always dreamed. Her hair was now long and dark and when she was playing she always wore it a stylish fashion. Her suntanned complexion suited her, and although she looked a little older was very attractive. She had been on several dates, but none led to lasting relationships, because as far as she was concerned the tour now took priority. Also she had never met anyone who she felt would be prepared to accept the close relationship that she had with Abe and Maria, as she now regarded them as her family. Although Rosa had tried and was still trying, she had no news of her parents or her old tutor and this caused her so much anguish at times.

Now she was about to go on tour, Rosa spent a lot of her free time practicing, so the packing and preparation was left to Maria. New clothes had to be bought, for she had an image to maintain whilst performing and in private. She was lucky that she was fairly tall, had a good figure, was attractive and could carry herself well, in fact she was very elegant, which considering what she had endured in the past was marvellous.

When the time came for them to depart they all shed a tear or two for Israel, which had been good to them, and all said that one-day they would return. As they sat in first class in the plane that was to take them to the USA, they compared their imminent departure with that of their arrival in Israel as immigrants on the boat, only a few years earlier.

The plane journey was very comfortable, and the accommodation in New York was the best. She had a few days to rest after the journey and to rehearse with the orchestra prior to her concert. In what little spare time she had, Rosa and Maria enjoyed themselves taking in the sights and shops of New York, which helped to dispel any pre-concert nerves. The concert was held in a huge auditorium, and the acoustics were wonderful, as were the orchestra and conductor. After the first rehearsal she knew she would be fine, so her first night nerves were soon dispelled and she a standing ovation and many floral tributes. The conductor gave a speech, which was unusual, and said how much he had enjoyed her performance. He was sorry that her tutor could not be here to hear her play, as she had been trained by one of the finest violinists the world had ever known. Sadly he had perished in one of the Nazi death camps during the war. At least now she knew what had become of him, when she heard what the conductor had just said she was filled with remorse, but could not show it at that moment.

Next day the music critics in the city press were unanimous in their reviews. She revelled in their praise, and the more she performed in front of large audiences the better she became. Although she was half expecting the truth of what had happened to her old tutor, it had still come as a shock to her, and that night, when alone, she cried herself to sleep, for she had first hand knowledge of what life and death meant in those camps. She thought of how kind, patient and considerate he had been to her when she first went to Paris. Her thoughts then turned to her parents; she consoled herself that at least they had been in England, and not Europe, when she had last seen them.

As for David, he had hardly figured in her thoughts; if he had survived the war, he was most likely married with a family, repairing bicycles. She had been hurt that he had not even bothered to come to the station to say goodbye to her when she had left for France, he probably had not thought of her again, and why should he? He was a gentile and she was a Jew, and "oil and water don't mix," as her Daddy used to say.

It was while she was thinking of David, that Maria said, 'A penny for your thoughts Rosa. You seemed to be so far away, or are they worth more than a penny?' As they had a little time to spare, Maria made a cup of tea. Rosa then related how she and David had met, how he had a cart and then a shop in the days when money was short. She told her how he had come to her home for tea, and how he had made such an impression on her parents.

'He must have been quite a young man, this David,' answered Maria, 'it's a pity I never met him, but I am sure he was nice and most likely neither you or I will meet him again now.' They finished their drinks, and David was never mentioned again.

The American tour finally came to an end, and the trio were on their way to Canada. They enjoyed their new found lifestyle, even though the travelling was tiring, especially for Rosa who had to practise constantly and perform every night. Her fame seemed to precede her wherever she went, and she was warmly welcomed in each city. The Canadian tour went from coast-to-coast, taking in all the main cities. As they travelled, they noticed that Eastern Canada was more European in the layout of its streets and roads, and all the houses were painted white, with quite a few having aluminium coloured roofs. As they got further west, the houses were stained and appeared darker, and were mainly constructed of timber, which was plentiful in Canada. As they travelled from province to province, the vast expanse of the country reminded Rosa, Abe and Maria of their journey to Poland and Russia. The Canadian tour was a huge success, and Rosa's agent said that there were many requests for her to return both there and to America in the near future.

Abe and Maria supported Rosa in every way: Maria acted as Rosa's dresser, and took a great weight off of Rosa's shoulders at times. Rosa paid Abe and Maria a good salary, their accommodation was always provided and all three had a good relationship, which worked very well. Rosa had quite a large wardrobe now with many evening gowns, but for some reason she never had a red gown.

The tour continued and they visited many countries. Spring soon passed into summer, and summer into late autumn, and the trio took a vacation in Israel before starting a tour of Europe during the winter.

Once back in Israel they had so many friends and places to visit, and as usual the weather was good to them. Rosa had promised to play a charity concert before starting the European tour, which was to take in quite a few cities in England and France. It seemed a lifetime since she had been to England, and realised that it would not be the same place as when she was last there. She had been much younger then, had her parents to care for her, and David when she needed him. In those far off days she had seemed so happy and until she left for France she had nothing but happy memories of England and its people. Although she had not spent much time in France before the war, she had enjoyed her time there, but she could not say the same once France was occupied, and especially later when she was taken prisoner. She wondered what her true feelings would be when she returned to Paris.

Every time she washed, she saw the tattoo on her arm, and it was a grim reminder that would never disappear from her body or mind. She always said that she would never have it surgically removed, as it was a constant reminder of what the Germans had done to her: she had no name, just a number. Wherever she played now, and in the future, she would never cover it up or try to hide it, she was not ashamed, and wanted the whole world to see it and be reminded, as she was, of those terrible days and nights, and what it stood for.

The vacation in Israel passed all to quickly. The spare time the three had was spent on the beach in and out of the water.

Rosa always wore a full swimsuit to cover the burn marks on her body, and no one seemed to take any notice of the three people who were really enjoying their free time, and Rosa really appreciated this.

The holiday in Israel, although short, was more than welcome and all three were feeling more relaxed, and although they seemed to spend so much time in each other's company, tempers did not seem to fray very often. Rosa was never temperamental like so many top artistes, and this helped to make life easier for all concerned.

The European tour was to start in France and then proceed to Belgium, Spain, Germany and then finish in England, where the first and last performance would be in London. And then she would return to North America and Canada. The short vacation in Israel was just what Rosa had needed, and she told her agent that when the European tour finished, she might postpone the North American tour in order to recharge her batteries. As she had had such a hectic year, her agent agreed.

Europe's top cities were more or less back to their pre-war grandeur, as most had not endured wartime bombing like Germany and England had. The weather was good, and all in all it promised to be a good tour.

When they reached Paris, Rosa overcame the painful memories of her arrest and interrogation there, and showed great resilience and strength of character in giving a triumphant performance. A weaker person could never have performed there as she did, but that was Rosa and full credit to her.

One morning, when Rosa was tuning her violin and practising scales, she saw Maria pull a face. She smiled as she turned, and said, 'Sorry, but you know that this practice is necessary.'

'I realise that my dear, I know I never would have made a violinist.'

Rosa stood as if transfixed for a moment, and then started to play. When she had finished, Maria said, 'What a lovely tune, I have never heard you playing that before, what is it called?'

'"Fascination", and it's the first time I have played it for a very long time. The last time I played it was when I was much younger, and David first came to visit at my home. You know Maria, the look on his face when I had finished playing suited the name of the piece of music, for if anyone appreciated, he did, for he was fascinated.'

'You never say much about David, but I know what an impression he made on you and your parents, and I guess it is as hard to forget him and so hard for anyone to match up with him. Sometimes I see you in deep thought and wonder what you are thinking about, but I never enquire. Sometimes it is nice to reminisce and go back in time and think what might have been, if times and places had been different.'

'How right you are Maria,' said Rosa, 'pity we can't always plan our lives as we plan a journey or a holiday, but that's life. If David is alive and well and is married, I'm sure he will have made some woman very happy.'

The door opened and Abe entered the room, 'Women's talk?' he asked, 'I hope I am not being discussed, as I do try to please but don't always succeed.'

'Go on with you,' said Maria, 'Go and make Rosa and I a cup of tea, we are thirsty with talking so much. You know Rosa wouldn't swap you.'

'Maybe there are many ladies out there who would like me,' he answered with a smile.

'Wishful thinking on your part,' said Maria, giving him a small push as he went past.

After her first performance, Rosa could enjoy Paris as she did when she had first arrived there many years ago. Although she tried to find many of her old friends, she had no success, and this made her very despondent as she realised so many must have perished. It was then that she knew that Paris and France could never be the same to her again, and it took the edge off the rest of her stay.

The orchestras and conductors she was playing with were the best, and they enhanced her performances. With each country's concerts behind her, her thoughts centred on visiting England, and returning home. As each new day dawned she became more excited about her visit. There was so much she wanted to show Abe and Maria in England, as neither of them had been before. After her vivid descriptions of her homeland, they were eager to visit, and she hoped that they would not be disappointed.

*****

David had continued to work hard. There never seemed enough hours in the day and once he had finalised a project there was always another in the pipeline. So far all he attempted had proved successful, and the larger the project the more he seemed to excel. His workforce was large and he never lost a moment's interest in what he was doing, be it site work, office work or finance, indeed he had a very busy and interesting business, and one his parents would have been most proud of.

One day when he was in a meeting with the Colonel and the board, David suggested that as the company was in a good financial position and there was little bomb damage left to clear in London, that they should look for further business interests. After seeing the motorways that had been built in pre-war Germany, David believed that England would soon follow suit, and would need a similar road network, especially now that the motor vehicle was becoming more popular, and more goods were being transported by road. David said that he would let the car industry people take charge of building the vehicles and they would take care of building the roads.

The Colonel thought the idea was a good one, and said that once again the bank would be required to provide some financial assistance, but if it proved as successful and profitable as their previous ventures, he did not think that there would be any opposition. No doubt there would also be grants from the government that would help the venture. The Colonel gave David a sly wink, and he knew why the Colonel wasn't called "the sly old fox" for nothing.

When the meeting came to an end, and most of the members had departed, Colonel Tate suggested that David stay and have a chat as there were one or two points he wished to discuss. When they were alone he said, 'I think that you should slow down a wee bit David; I think you are pushing yourself too hard. You are still a young man, try and enjoy yourself more, don't burn yourself out and give the undertaker a job just yet. I may not be your CO anymore, but I'm giving you an order now. Slow down.'

'Very good sir,' answered David with a smile, 'I'll try.'

'No try about it, I have given you an order, understand?'

'Yes sir,' said David, jokingly saluting him. 'I knew we had a meeting today so I arranged to have some flowers delivered. Would you take them to Mrs Tate and ask her when it would be convenient for you both to take up my invitation to a show and dinner, as I did enjoy your company the last time we were together.'

'So did I, and I am sure she did too,' he answered, 'thank you very much, very thoughtful of you and much appreciated I can assure you.'

Later that night when they had taken their evening meal and were very comfortable in the lounge, Laura remarked to the Colonel how thoughtful it was of David to send her roses, especially as he had remembered that they were her favourite flowers. It was then that the Colonel told her of David's latest idea.

'We could certainly do with a much better road system, and if he does get started on the venture I'm sure that he will get very involved. I really did enjoy helping to design the interior of the hotel, but I hope he does not want me to use a spade, or mix concrete for the new motorway. Tell him so next time you meet him anyway. I'll phone him or drop him a line to thank him for the flowers, and the invitation for the night out he has so generously offered.'

'Somehow I can't see you mixing concrete my dear, maybe mixing a cake but not concrete. I can't see it being your forte can you?'

Both laughed, they had a good sense of humour, which blended well with each other's.

'Anyway, I'm pleased he has no designs on you, or you him my dear,' said the Colonel.

'Taking a lot for granted dear aren't you?' she said, giving him a sly look as she rose from where they were sitting, then remarked, 'Maybe it is time I made you a little jealous, could be that you have taken things for granted a little too much over the years. Now that has given you something to think about hasn't it.' She then turned, bent over and gave him kiss as he sat there.

David had to go to Paris on business not long after his meeting with the Colonel and the board. Whilst walking through Paris he glanced up at a poster on one of the billboards that had been defaced, it was the face of a woman, but part of the face was missing, and it appeared she was holding a violin. Being in French he could not understand it; he could speak a little French that he had picked up in his service days, like so many had during the war, but he could not read French. He didn't stop to take a closer look, and never thought that it could be advertising Rosa's concert, even though he was in Paris.

Once his business was completed he quickly returned back to London and the hotel that was now his home. The staff in the hotel were always aware of his presence, and this kept them on their toes; as a result, the hotel and its staff had acquired a reputation as being one of the best in the city.

When he often travelled up and down the country on business he usually went in his chauffeur driven limousine, this meant that he had more opportunities to view the countryside and decide where he would like to build his new home. He had never forgotten the night when he first saw the dancers in the house as a child, and how he had looked back down the drive and thought to himself that one day he would have a house like that. The time for the realisation of this dream had arrived much quicker than he had ever imagined, even though it had taken a war and so much personal loss to achieve it. The countryside appealed to him more than London, with its hectic and busy lifestyle, which seemed to take up so much of his time now. He wanted a quiet place where he could escape. The countryside in his native Yorkshire was some of the best in England, and if and when the motorways were constructed, it would become so much closer to London, and this gave him food for thought.

The government of the day must have had similar thoughts to David regarding the new motorways, for it was not long before the Colonel phoned him asking for a meeting. David was surprised to hear that it was the Colonel who had set the wheels in motion, and he was now realising just how powerful Colonel Tate was, not just in finance and banking circles, but also as a man in grey. Of course the Minister of State would take credit for the idea, but David knew who the ultimate winner would be in the long run, and once again his idea looked like coming to fruition. He thought, not bad for an elementary school education, at least he had been taught the three Rs and manners, honesty and common sense. His teacher may have given him sore hands for dreaming, but at least most of his dreams over the years had paid dividends, both for him and others.

* * * * *

One day when Ted arrived home from the hospital, he and Nancy sat discussing their respective day's work. He asked her if she would like to go to London for a few days as he had a medical meeting to attend, which would take up most of his time during the day, but he would have the evenings free so that they could dine out and go to see a show at the theatre. She could visit shops, and maybe Gail would be able to spend a few hours with her one day.

'Thanks my love,' she answered, 'what a marvellous idea, and I promise not to spend too much money in the shops. When are we likely to go, and where will we be staying?'

'I will confirm the actual date tomorrow. The accommodation is at a new large hotel, which has only recently been completed. I'm told it's excellent in every way. When I know the actual date I'll contact Gail, and I'm sure she will manage to pay us a visit whilst we are there.'

When Ted knew the date of the London visit, he contacted Gail who said she was free to join them and would look forward to seeing them.

Both Ted and Nancy were very busy over the next few weeks and the time for the visit to London soon arrived. They enjoyed their journey down to London in the car, and as they had ample time they shared the driving. When they arrived they were amazed at the size of the hotel, and once inside were even more amazed by the ambience of the interior, and were delighted to be staying there. As they booked in, Ted remarked that if their room and food lived up to these standards, then it would be alright for him, and gave a small chuckle. When they saw their room, and later on had a meal, both were more than satisfied. Later on that evening when they were taking coffee in the lounge, they discussed the hotel. They wondered who had built and designed such an elegant building; little knowing that David was responsible for so much of it.

Nancy and Gail met up the next day, enjoyed the shops and found lots to talk about. When lunchtime came, they found somewhere close by to eat, and Nancy told Gail all about her wonderful hotel. Gail said that it had not been open long; it had been built by a large company who had cleared a lot of bombsites, and rebuilt office blocks, shops and hotels on them. The company's maintenance equipment and trucks could be seen on the streets, all had a peculiar motif on the side, an odd sort of thing, something like a small cart or truck. Many people were puzzled when they saw it, as no one seemed to know what it represented, and there was never a name or address on anything.

The restaurant was busy at lunchtime; sitting at a reserved table not far from Nancy and Gail was a lady and gentleman. The lady was in the direct line of vision from Nancy, but was too far away to hear Nancy and Gail's conversation. When Nancy had finished eating and was waiting for her next course, she remarked in a low voice how elegant the lady looked, so smart and attractive in every way. Gail replied that she and a friend had been to a concert a short time ago and that the lady in question was the international violinist, who was on a world tour, and the gentleman was the conductor. She was in London for a short while, before continuing her tour. Gail suggested that Nancy should try and obtain a ticket for one of her concerts, for she was marvellous to listen to.

Nancy and Gail finished their meal and went on their way, as there were so many shops for Nancy to visit in her short stay in London, and so far she had not spent a lot of money.

CHAPTER 16

WHEN NANCY AND GAIL had finished their afternoon shopping they took a taxi back to Nancy's hotel. Gail wanted to see her father, and Nancy wanted to show her the hotel. When they passed the ballroom, the door was ajar, and they were able to see inside, both were impressed with what they saw, 'Care for a dance Mum?'

As they turned and walked to the lift to take them to their room, Gail said, 'You and Dad don't do much dancing do you? It's years since I saw you dance; do you think you can remember how?'

'Maybe if I had the right partner,' she replied, not wishing to explain how she and David had danced that night away and how she had enjoyed it and the way he had held her close to him, so much. As they were in the lift she wondered whether she should still meet David in December as they had planned, or be content with this visit to London with Ted and Gail. These thoughts soon disappeared as the lift door opened and they were on their floor. They settled in the room, rang for room service and ordered afternoon tea for a little later, as Ted would be back from his meeting shortly.

When Ted and Gail met they had such a lot to talk over and Nancy hardly got a word in edgeways. She just sat there pouring the tea and feeling very content seeing Gail and Ted so close. Ted had always loved and spoilt Gail, and seeing them as she saw them now, thought she must never hurt either one of them if possible. It was while they were sat talking that Nancy said they had seen the international violinist in the restaurant at lunchtime, and how smart she appeared, and according to Gail how well she played. She asked Ted if he could get tickets for her performance, as she would like to hear her play as they both liked good music. Ted said his seminar would be over by late morning, he would meet Nancy and they would try and obtain some tickets, as sometimes there were some available due to cancellations. They went down for an evening meal in the hotel, and Gail complimented the standards of the food and hotel before she left.

Later when Nancy and Ted retired, Ted soon fell asleep, but somehow the lady in the restaurant had made an impression on Nancy, but she had no idea why, after all she was a stranger. It had been a fairly hectic day and after a little while Nancy fell asleep in the sumptuous bed.

Next day, the seminar finished early, Ted met Nancy, they spent a pleasant day together and were fortunate in obtaining tickets for the evening's concert, which was even better than Gail had described. Ted said how elegant the solo violinist looked on stage, he had never heard a violin played so marvellously, no wonder she was world class. The programme was fairly light, and everyone there seemed to enjoy the evening very much.

When they returned to the hotel they did not go straight up to their room, but went into the huge lounge for a nightcap. It was while they were sitting there enjoying their drink and admiring the surroundings that Ted said, 'You know Nancy, I think I could get used to this lifestyle. I could stay here and take in all that London has to offer, how about you, don't you agree?'

As she looked at him her face lit up with one of her bright, open smiles, 'Maybe for a little while, but I guess I should soon miss my lovely home, my garden and flowers. The flowers here are beautiful and I do appreciate them so, but when I see what the Lord and I have produced at home, I think I appreciate mine a little more. Please don't think I am being ungrateful, I am not. I have enjoyed every minute here in London and would love to do it all again soon, including this magnificent hotel, but you know that I am not an envious person and I am more than satisfied with the lifestyle I have, thank you.'

Even though there were several people in the room, Ted bent forward and kissed her saying, 'That is one of the many reasons why I love you so, my darling.'

She kind of blushed and then said 'Ted, stop it, people will think we are having an affair and I'm a scarlet woman.'

'Let them think what they like,' he announced. 'I know you're not and never could be and that is all that matters to me. Aren't I lucky in having you for my wife.' They got up, left the lounge and went up to their room.

Ted soon fell asleep but not Nancy, she lay and could not seem to clear her mind. Why had David asked her to go and see him in London, and why had she agreed to go to him? It was only for a few hours and she knew that they would not be intimate, so why should it bother her so? Since she had known Ted, there had never been any other man in her life, nor had she ever wanted one, so why did she want to see David? She did so want to go to him, even if it was only for a few hours. After much soul searching she eventually fell asleep.

In the morning after a good breakfast they were soon on their way back home, and back to their normal lifestyle. December would soon be here, and she would have to decide whether she would go back to London for the day or cancel the meeting. The more she thought of it the more she wondered which of the two of them would be the most disappointed if she did not go. It did not seem a lot to ask as a Christmas present, a few hours of someone's company, but she could not tell Ted who she was going to visit and why she was going to London alone. She did not want to deceive Ted, he did not deserve that, not even for one day a year. After all, she was a married woman and not a silly love sick teenager, and the sooner she realised that the better it would be for all concerned, more so herself, as she had so much to lose.

Gail came home for a weekend soon after Ted and Nancy returned from London. She said that she had a new boyfriend, and she hoped that they could meet him soon. She also said that while they were in a restaurant she had seen David, they had not spoken as he was leaving and had not noticed them.

He was alone and looked very well. Her boyfriend had said that he had seen his face in the papers but could not remember when and where, it was for something important, but not a scandal.

'I thought you'd be interested to hear about him Mum,' Gail concluded.

'You know I'm interested Gail, it's only female curiosity, isn't it? I hope for his sake it is to his advantage, as he seemed a nice sort of young man, and your Uncle Paul always spoke well of him. He was a perfect gentleman when he and Paul came to stay for those few days leave during the war, and at Paul's wedding.'

Until Gail had mentioned David to Nancy she had almost made up her mind not to go to London and meet him in December, but now he had been in the papers she was now very interested to find out more about his private life if she could. She knew so very little about him, only that he carried a torch for some Jewish woman, and of course for her. He had stayed at her home, met her husband and her daughter, knew of her lifestyle, in fact quite a lot about her and yet, she knew so very little about him. If they did meet as arranged and got into conversation, she may yet discover a little of his background and his life both now and in the past.

When Gail had left and Nancy was alone with her thoughts, she knew deception or no deception; she had to meet David in the near future, if only to find out a little about his life. Also if they did share a kiss, it was not being unfaithful to Ted, not in the sense of being unfaithful; she would be home by bed time and it would put a little sparkle into her otherwise dull life. Now she had finally made her mind to go she felt more at ease with herself and it showed. Before David and she had parted at the wedding, he had given her a phone number to call him anytime during the day.

When Ted came home from work one day, Nancy said that she would like to go to London before Christmas maybe to do some shopping. She would go on her own one day when

151

Ted was at work, she would be home by bedtime, and what did he think of the idea?

'Would you mind, Ted?'

'Of course not my dear. I don't ask you when I go golfing for the day do I? By all means you go and enjoy yourself, but come back safe to me. Are you sure you don't want to stay the night?'

'Thanks all the same, but I shall be back the same day, its just a few hours away and I want to do some shopping.'

'I remember you said quite a while ago that you hoped to have a day in London in December,' answered Ted, 'so go.'

The next day, after Ted had gone to work, Nancy phoned the number that David had given her. A female answered the phone, and when Nancy asked if Mr Jones was available she was told that he was out on business, and who was speaking? Was there any message? And could they ring her back if she gave them a number? Nancy asked if he would be back later that day, and if so at what time, then she would call again. After a short pause, the voice said that if she could ring back at 3.30pm he should be available. Nancy did not want to give her number, as she did not want to sow any seeds of suspicion. She had no idea whether the person she had been speaking was David's wife, girlfriend or partner.

After 3.30pm she picked up the phone, dialled the same number, which was answered by the same female voice as before. Nancy asked if Mr Jones was available, when asked who was speaking, replied just a friend. When David answered he asked to whom he was speaking and realised that it was Nancy, his voice changed; it was not a business voice he was using now, but a softer more personal tone, and when Nancy suggested a date for them to meet in the very near future his face broke into a huge smile. When the conversation came to an end, he turned to his secretary and instructed her to keep that day free of any business commitments in his diary. As it was coming up to Christmas and the festive season approaching the secretary did not think anything about the phone conversation Mr Jones had just received.

When the day arrived for Nancy to go to London she arose fairly early, prepared breakfast for Ted and herself, did a quick tidy up before getting ready to go to London. When Ted saw her as she entered the room he remarked how nice she looked, then as a joke he added, 'You always do to me my love.'

'Nice of you to say it anyway,' she replied, 'and thank you.'

Ted took her to the station and she gave him a quick kiss before boarding the carriage.

It was lovely weather for December, more like spring, and she was pleased, as it made the journey more pleasant. The train was on time and David was on the platform to meet her; both gave a huge smile as they walked to greet one another, and held each other close and tight. Almost the first thing that David said to her was, 'There is a Father Christmas and he has delivered my present early, the one present that I wanted the most. Thank you for coming Nancy.' When she heard him say this she was so pleased that she had changed her mind and come to London to meet him. As they walked the station platform, David said how well she looked and how nice and smart she was. She laughed as she said, 'It is still morning and I have already been told twice how nice I look. The ticket collector also gave me a nice smile, but I put that down to the perfume I was wearing.' Then arm in arm they walked to the station entrance both looking so happy. David hailed a taxi, and they were soon on their way to spend those precious hours together. The taxi took them to one of the London parks, and when they had alighted David said, 'I did not think you would be suitably dressed for cycle riding today my dear, but that cycle ride is as vivid in my mind as if it were yesterday: the pink dress, the pink sandals, your hair loose and free and even the bottle of water that we shared.'

'Fancy you remembering all that,' answered Nancy, and she gave his arm a little squeeze.

'There is so very little I cannot remember about you since we first met,' he replied, 'and I'm sure I never will.'

As they walked in the park, David asked Nancy so many questions about Ted, Gail and herself. With the questions flowing, the time in the park went all too quickly. When Nancy asked about his early life, David told her of his childhood, family, how he had always been interested in business and how he had met Rosa. He then told Nancy that he had spent much more time with her than he had ever spent with Rosa. Before he could say more, she asked him if he had found out anything about this Rosa, his Jewess, or was she still missing from his life? She hoped she was not being too inquisitive to cause offence, as that was the last thing she wished to do, as she valued his friendship so much. He told her how he had searched for Rosa across Europe when he had finished his army service, on the chance that it had been Rosa he had seen being deloused in the concentration camp, and how he had had no success in finding her. He now realised that he must have been wrong in thinking that it was her in the first place. He said that when he returned to England he had met up with a person that he had known in the services, and this person had been more than helpful to him in many ways since their first meeting, and that he would eternally be grateful to him.

David and Nancy walked from the park, where he hailed a taxi that took them to a very nice hotel where they ordered lunch. David said if she wished to do any shopping he would accompany her, as to take a lady shopping would be a change and a new experience for him. She answered, if she saw anything that caught her eye she may buy it, but she had really come to London, to spend the time with him and not to shop. He said that later in the afternoon he had a surprise for her, and that he had ordered an early evening dinner before she had to catch her train back home. While they were having lunch she said that she and Ted had been in London not too long ago, as Ted had had to attend a meeting. She remarked how London had been cleared and was now looking much better with new buildings, and how they had stayed in a marvellous new hotel, where the accommodation, food, décor and ambience were first class. She could thoroughly recommend it to him, so he must try it for himself in the future sometime. He did not tell her that he was or had been so involved in the course of its construction and the building and clearance of much of London. Being boastful was not in his nature, and Nancy still did not know much of his present life or really a great amount of his past life either. He had disclosed so very little about himself, so she realised that to enquire any further in that direction may cause him some embarrassment so she changed the subject in order not to spoil the day they were having together. To have searched for Rosa like he had done across Europe showed his true feelings and the calibre of the man, and if he had wanted her to know of his life he would have told her.

They enjoyed their lunch, which they did not hurry, then did some window-shopping; one shop window displayed some very smart clothes, but very expensive.

Nancy said, 'I think I'll try that dress, won't be a moment.'

'May I come with you?' he asked, 'I would really like to.'

'Certainly,' she replied, 'I have never had a male escort in a dress shop before,' and she laughed. She asked for the dress, took it into the changing room and emerged a moment later wearing the blue dress. It did suit her and she looked so very pretty in it. David looked, smiled and said to the assistant, 'Have you one in pink like it for the lady to try on?'

'Yes sir,' came the reply, 'won't be a moment.' She returned almost immediately and gave Nancy the pink dress, which she took into the changing room.

'I know why you want to see me in pink, David,' she said as she emerged from the changing room, 'Satisfied,' she asked with a smile, 'now which is it to be?'

David walked over to Nancy and said very quickly to her, so the assistant could not hear, 'Have them both as my Christmas present to you, you look lovely in both. I'll pay for them; they're my present for coming to me.'

'You will not pay for them,' she said most indignant, 'thanks for the offer, but they are very expensive so I will settle for one, the pink one, and Ted pays for my clothes.'

David did not argue, and left Nancy to pay for the dress and have it wrapped. When they were clear of the shop, Nancy said, 'I am so sorry David, I hope I have not offended you with what I have just said, I have just realised that what I said in haste, I now repent in leisure. It was most ungracious of me, and I hope you will forgive me, as I don't deserve your kindness and consideration, so if you would like to say cheerio to me here and now, I would understand and realise it is what I deserve.'

'Don't be silly,' answered David, 'if anything it is I who should be apologising to you for being so crass, and I promise to be more sensible in future.' Then with a smile, he said, 'I think the pink one suited you best. Come Nancy I have another surprise for you,' and with that he hailed a taxi.

One of the top London hotels had a tea dance, and as luck would have it, it was held on the day of Nancy's visit. The taxi took them to the hotel in minutes. The ballroom was nice, large and had a good stage with a live band playing some very good dance tunes. The dance was fairly well patronised, but there was ample room for dancing. When Nancy saw the dance in progress, her face lit up as she said, 'David, what a marvellous surprise you have kept for me, really I don't deserve the consideration and affection you show towards me.'

'Yes you do,' he replied, 'May I have the honour of the next dance please.' As they danced, Nancy's mind went back to their first dance all those years ago. They never missed a dance all afternoon, and when the band played the last waltz, it ended all too soon for them. David had booked an early dinner, which they both enjoyed, and gave them time to relax before Nancy had to go back to the station. After dinner they sat hand in hand taking coffee in the lounge, and both said how much they had enjoyed their day together.

The taxi came as ordered and the train was on time. Just before Nancy boarded the train, they held each other so close, and the farewell kiss seemed to mean such a lot to them. David thanked her very much for coming and said, 'A year is a long time to wait, but it was well worth waiting for, and I will be here next year if you will.'

Nancy said, 'I'm sorry that you have not found your Rosa yet, if it had been possible I would have given her to you as your Christmas present.' She knew that she would have been jealous of Rosa, but with a squeeze of his hand she was on the train and on her way back home to Ted.

Ted was there to meet her, and gave her a kiss on the cheek as she alighted. 'Had a good day my dear?' he asked.

'Yes thank you,' she replied, 'I have had a wonderful time, but I am tired and ready for bed.'

'I suppose you have had a busy day, so you can tell me all about London later.' Then taking her arm he escorted her to the car and they were on their way home.

David took a taxi back to his hotel. He had enjoyed his day very much and enjoyed the company of Nancy whenever they met.

* * * * *

Rosa, Abe and Maria were enjoying their stay in London so much that Rosa had not found the time to show them the rest of England, and with Christmas so near they had decided to put their intended tour on hold for the time being. She still practised everyday and the final performance of her tour, here in London.

One day Rosa had forgotten to put her St Christopher medallion back around her neck when she had finished in the bathroom. Maria found it, packed it in a suitcase, and thought no more about it. Later when Rosa realised that she was not wearing it she was so upset, she searched and searched and could not find it. When she asked Maria and Abe if they had seen it, Maria said she had found it, and had put it somewhere safe, but could not remember where she had put it. Rosa was so upset to have misplaced it, but Maria said that it would turn up soon and that she would do her best to remember where she had put it and would search until she found it, for she knew how much it meant to Rosa.

David also had his St Christopher medallion around his neck and was never without it. He still had his two army dog tags on it as he had throughout his war time days. As David was doing some Christmas shopping in London one day, he saw someone whom he thought he recognised, but before he could get a better view of her, she had disappeared in the crowds of people. Then when he was passing an advert for a concert, he somehow had a premonition to go, something he normally did not do. He decided he must attend the concert, which featured a solo female violinist from Israel by the name of Asor Enivel, a name that meant so little to him, but he could not seem to get the name from his mind.

He was very busy at work getting everything ready for the Christmas holiday, but did manage to book a seat for the concert. Then one night when he was alone, sat in his room the name Asor Enivel would not go away. It was then that he realised it was Rosa Levine spelt backwards. She was alive; it was definitely she whom he had seen in the store the other day and also in the death camp. The next morning he could not get through to his office quick enough to cancel his mornings appointments. He was desperate to find out where Rosa was staying.

When he arrived at Rosa's hotel, he was met by Maria, who told him that she was at the concert hall. He quickly explained that he was David, and that he and Rosa had been friends long ago. He told her that he had booked to go to the concert that night, and would send Rosa a bouquet of red roses. He asked Maria to present them with his medallion he would give her for safekeeping, but he must have it back after the presentation. He wanted Rosa to see the medallion on the roses. He asked Maria if Rosa had a red dress, and if so, could she be persuaded to wear it tonight with her hair loose, as that was how he remembered her playing Fascination to him long ago. He knew it was a lot to ask coming from a stranger, but he wanted to keep it a secret from Rosa, until she had finished her performance and then he would make himself known to her, if it were possible, from the wings of the stage.

Maria agreed to do all that David had asked if it was possible, even to the red dress. For some unknown reason Rosa had purchased a red dress not long ago and had never worn it. David thanked Maria very much, gave her the medallion then apologised that he did not have a case to put it in. When he said case, Maria immediately remembered where she had put Rosa's medallion - in a suitcase, which was in a closet. Before he departed, David asked Maria if she would be at the concert hall, and if so, he would probably see her later that evening, then shaking Maria's hand he departed.

Later that day he asked his secretary if it would be possible to cancel any appointments he had for the following day, he knew it was not giving her much notice and if anything was really urgent he would attend. When she checked she said that there was nothing really important, and with a cheeky smile said, 'You have my permission to take the day off work.'

'Thank you, I appreciate it,' he answered with a smirk, 'one day I'll do the same for you.'

When Rosa had finished her rehearsal that morning she was looking forward to her last concert, as it would allow her to relax a little and show Abe and Maria more of England. She wanted to take them to her old hometown, and hopefully she would find some news of her parents, be it pleasant or sad.

On her arrival home, Maria didn't tell Rosa that she had had a visitor that morning; she wanted Rosa to have the surprise of seeing David again. She also didn't mention it to Abe, which was unusual for she never kept a secret from him. All three were soon in conversation, Rosa told them that after her rehearsal she had enjoyed lunch with a friend, and had been window-shopping. Abe said that he too had enjoyed his day so far; he had been for a walk, had lunch and visited a picture gallery. 'How about you?' he asked looking at Maria, 'had a nice day?'

'Nice day,' she retorted. 'Its alright for some. Who do you think has done the ironing, washing, cooking, cleaning, putting things away, preparing for tonight's concert, not you two is it?' Her face then broke into a huge smile, 'Well if you two have enjoyed yourself, so have I, and it has been a pleasure doing the chores for you, as I know you both appreciate it. As both of you have had lunch, afternoon tea will have to suffice, as I have not had time to do much preparation for the concert this evening. Since you have not yet worn that new red ball gown, I was hoping that you would wear it tonight. Will that be OK Rosa?'

'Of course,' replied Rosa, 'it will go with my black shoes, and I have not worn red for such a long time.'

Before she could change her mind, Maria had left the room and put the red dress in the case for the evening performance, together with all the other things that Rosa required. Maria was Rosa's dresser, and it was not often that she forgot anything, for Rosa always changed before and after her performance in her dressing room. Maria also told Abe that he must go to the concert tonight without fail, she was making sure that everything would be as David had requested, and Abe had yet to be introduced to David.

Maria took the case from the closet, took out the medallion, and put it with the one that David had given her in the envelope. David had told Maria that he was sending some

160

roses to Rosa, and that these would be delivered to the concert hall at the end of the performance. He wanted to make sure that the medallions would be placed on the roses when they were presented to Rosa.

When they finished their conversation, Rosa said she was going to have a bath and get ready for the concert. Abe helped Maria to clear away and then sat and read for a little while. When Rosa was dressed and ready to go, she turned and said to Maria, 'I have enjoyed today so much, I'm so lucky'

Maria gave her one of her looks, and answered, 'I am so pleased for you my dear. Now let us hope that the concert goes well, and that the day ends fine for you, as I have a feeling it will.'

'Oh you and your feelings,' answered Rosa, with a smile and gave Maria a hug.

Being the last concert of the tour, the concert hall was full to overflowing, such was the popularity of the conductor, orchestra and of course Rosa. When they arrived, Rosa and Maria went to the star dressing room. Rosa changed, did her make up, and waited for Maria to do her hair as she always did. Normally she did it up in a bun at the back of her head, which was kept in place by many pins. As she brushed the long dark tresses she said, 'I'm afraid I forgot the hairpins for your hair. Do you mind if you wear your hair down tonight my dear?'

'Of course not,' said Rosa, 'it'll make a change.'

As they looked in the large dressing mirror, Maria said, 'I think it makes you look younger when you wear it loose.'

Rosa had several changes of ball gown throughout the concert, and Maria made sure that she would wear the red one last as David had asked. Rosa tuned her violin, and prepared herself for when she was called to go on stage.

David left his hotel in good time, for he did not wish to be late. He had managed to get a good seat with a splendid view. The orchestra played marvellously, and the concert hall showed their appreciation with a rapturous round of applause. When Rosa came on the stage, there was no mistaking that she was his Rosa, here in the flesh. She played superbly, world class, and the audience knew it. She certainly looked fine and well.

In the interval he asked the management if he could stand in the wings while Rosa finished her performance, and also, if she would play as a final request, just for him, the piece of music Fascination. He explained to them briefly about his relationship with Rosa, and they said that they would do everything in their power to make his request possible, even providing the orchestra with the music for Fascination and keeping things secret until the last minute.

When the time came for the final piece, the audience certainly showed their appreciation. Rosa looked magnificent in her red dress, just like she had done when she had played for David as a young girl. When she had finished playing, floral tributes started to arrive on the stage. Finally David's was given to her, and as she saw the medallions on the roses, her eyes filled with tears, as she knew exactly who had sent them. The conductor had been forewarned of David's request, and when Rosa had composed herself for a moment, he turned to the audience, and said he had a request from somebody very dear to her, asking her to play Fascination. Rosa agreed, and never did she play with such emotion, it was as if the old violin and she were one. When the music ended the audience gave a standing ovation; when he could restore quiet to the hall, the conductor said that he felt that both he and the audience had been very privileged to have been in the concert hall that evening and heard that last piece of music being played so marvellously. He had never heard such a performance before and he doubted if he ever would again. Then as Rosa turned to the wings, she saw David standing there. When she had the chance, she hurried from the stage to David, flinging herself into his arms, and holding and squeezing him so tight. Maria and Abe soon joined them and they all went to her dressing room, the room soon filled with well-wishers, and it was quite a while before the four were all alone.

Rosa introduced David to Abe and Maria. Maria gave a smile and said that they had met previously, and it was then that he had given her his St Christopher medallion, to present to Rosa. After quite a while David asked Rosa if she would like to go with him back to his hotel, as they had so much to catch up on and talk about. Abe and Maria said that they would attend to the dresses and Rosa's personal belongings, and see them safely back to their hotel. Rosa soon changed back into her suit and blouse, and as she and David were leaving the room she laughed and said, Please don't wait up for me, I will see you when I see you, and I'm sure that David will take good care of me.'

Once outside the hall David hailed a taxi and they were on their way to his hotel. The hotel that Rosa was staying at whilst in London was good, but nothing on a par to the hotel she was now entering. Once inside the suite of rooms that David used, he picked up the phone and asked for a light supper for two, together with a bottle of the best champagne. Rosa sat down on the huge sofa, which was most comfortable, and almost before they could gather themselves there was a knock at the door. After a slight hesitation the door opened and in walked a waiter, looking immaculate. He moved the coffee table nearer to the settee, laid the food from his large trolley onto the table and said that he hoped everything would be satisfactory, and should they require anything further they just had to ring. David thanked him and he left the room.

The food looked wonderful and the chef had excelled himself. Rosa said that the food looked so appetising that she was sure that she would enjoy it. David remarked how wonderful it was to see her sitting there; it was something that he thought he would never see again.

When they had finished David filled Rosa's glass with some more champagne and sat down opposite her in a large armchair. Rosa looked across at him and said, 'I feel so comfortable now, thank you so much David.' The conversation started as they had so much to tell one another.

David said that he had stood in the background at the station as she had left for France, and waited, waving until the train was out of sight. As she held out her arms to him and beckoned him to come nearer, David noticed the tattoo on her arm around her shoulder.

'Oh Rosa it was you I saw in that camp holding that bundle of rags close to you. I tried so hard to find you. When I finished my Army service I travelled halfway across Europe and the Baltic in the hope of finding you, but to no avail.'

Looking at David she said with a sob in her voice and a tear on her cheek, 'Thank you so very much for telling me that, it means so much to me and something I shall never forget. Please don't change from the David that I have always known.'

It was not early when the concert had finished, and with the supper and the talking, time slipped by, and when dawn came they were still sitting side by side on the settee. With the emotions of the previous day, the champagne and the warmth of the hotel, they fell asleep in each other's arms.

They awoke almost together, and both smiled. David asked if Rosa would like to use the bathroom first. David then showered, dressed and then came into the lounge and rang for breakfast, which they ate in his room. Whilst they were having breakfast they picked up the conversation from the previous night. Rosa said that she hoped that David would not mind the many questions which she kept putting to him. Before breakfast was finished, Rosa asked if there was a Mrs Jones or a lady friend in his life at present? She did not think that there was a Mrs Jones, as if there had been she would not have been asked her back to his hotel. He told her that there was no Mrs Jones or had been, and when they had more time he would tell her all about his private life, but there was too much to disclose over breakfast, and as soon as it was finished he wanted to take her out for the day and spoil her as much as possible. He asked her to phone Abe and Maria, to tell them that he would return her to them before midnight, but today she was his. She was looking forward to spending the whole day with him; it would be the happiest day of her life.

The weather was fine and bright and as they walked along the London streets, it was hard to tell which of the two was enjoying the others' company the most. When they were having lunch, David asked Rosa if she would be spending Christmas in London, as Christmas was not too far away and her next engagement was not until the New Year. Rosa told him how Abe, Maria and herself had first met and that she now considered them her family, as they had been so good to her, when she had needed help the most. She told him that she had had one or two male friends in the past, and had enjoyed herself but nothing had been serious for long, possibly music was to blame, as it played such an important part in her life and had done so for so long. Then with a laugh she said that being a Jew did not always help.

David looked at his watch and then said, 'I guess it's time we made a move. Do you think that we will ever catch up on explaining all the years that we have been apart?'

Before it was time for them to say goodbye, David asked Rosa if she would like to spend Christmas with him at his hotel. He was almost certain that he could find accommodation for Abe and Maria, two rooms did not seem a lot to ask of the hotel even though it would be the festive season, and he knew the management fairly well. If she would accept his invitation then it would be delighted for them to be guests, but if she had a previous invitation, or had made alternative arrangements then he would understand. Rosa replied that as they had not made any previous arrangements, and she was sure that all three of them would love to accept his invitation to spend Christmas with him.

The rest of the day passed all too quickly for them. When at last it was time to say goodbye at Rosa's hotel, he said that he could not have had a more enjoyable day and thanked

Rosa so much. He told her he would be in contact with her by phone tomorrow. He said that due to pressure from business, he could not spend more time with her, but that he would make sure that he would see more of her after the next few days. As they were standing in the foyer of Rosa's hotel that was full of people, David kissed her on the cheek and said goodbye so as not to embarrass her.

Rosa went straight from the lift to Abe and Maria's room; they had waited up for her and wanted to know how she and David had got on. She told them how she and David had talked so much, how the time had flown, how they had fallen asleep on the settee, what a wonderful day she had shared with him and what a magnificent hotel he lived in. She also said that he was single, but had not said what he did for a profession, in fact he had not disclosed much about his private life, past or present, in most of their conversation. He had told her he would tell all at a later meeting, which she said, knowing David, he would. Both Abe and Maria agreed what a nice person he appeared to be, and liked the idea of spending Christmas with him in order to get to know him better.

David was able to arrange two rooms for his guests, and made sure that they were very near to his own suite. When he next phoned Rosa, he told her that the accommodation was in place for Christmas, and could she have dinner with him every evening until she came there to stay at his hotel or any other restaurant of her choice.

Over dinner one night, David told Rosa his life story since they had last seen each other. He told her about the cycle shop, the army and the death of his parents. He also told her about the week he had spent at Nancy's home and the time that they spent together: cycle riding, gardening, the dance and how he had fallen in love with her, but she was married, and then during the war how he had met up with Nancy's husband Ted and how he had saved his friend's arm. He then recalled how they had met again at Paul's wedding and of their decision to meet in London once a year, which they had shared only a few days ago unbeknown to her husband. He said that they had never been intimate, and never would be, as he had too much respect for her and her husband. The most that they ever shared was a kiss when they parted, that they had agreed to meet just one day every year.

He then told Rosa how he had met his Colonel after the war had ended, and about the ideas he had which came into fruition with the Colonel's help, money, hard work and luck. He said, 'I have been lucky, for I have found you again, something that money could never have bought me,' and he gave her hand a squeeze.

Giving David a smile she said, 'We have both been lucky to survive the war and its horrors, and to be here enjoying this marvellous meal together.'

Christmas Eve soon came and Rosa, Abe and Maria arrived at David's hotel for their Christmas stay. David was out, doing his last minute shopping, so was not there to greet them when they arrived. Both Abe and Maria were very impressed with the hotel, and even more than pleased when they saw their rooms.

When David returned, he apologised for not being there when they arrived, and hoped they approved of their rooms. They agreed to get ready and meet up for dinner. Having dined there previously, Rosa knew that the food would be excellent, and made Abe and Maria very hungry when she talked about the meal that she had enjoyed there last time.

The four of them enjoyed their meal and when it was over retired to the lounge for coffee. The conversation flowed easily, and it was as though they had known each other for years. After a while David asked if they would like to go to the ballroom where a dance was in progress. The ballroom looked a picture, whoever had decorated it for the festive holidays had done a very good job. The dance floor was fairly full; the live band played well, and everyone present was having a good time. They found a table and David ordered drinks.

When the next dance started, David asked Maria, 'Would

you care for a waltz?'

'I would love to; I've not danced for years. Abe and I never seem to have time for dancing.'

She and David soon found the tempo once they were on the floor, and did not disgrace each other. When they returned to the table, Maria commented on what a good dancer David was, but she apologised that she wasn't up to his standard.

'You will find a difference dancing with me,' said Rosa smiling at David, 'that is if you would be kind enough to ask me to dance?'

'I would love to dance with you,' said David.

He then pulled her to her feet and led her to the dance floor. He held her to him so secure and firm, yet so tender and gentle, just as he had done when he danced with Nancy. Although Rosa was not as good a dancer, he knew that she was enjoying herself so much, and that with practice she would make an excellent dance partner. When it came for the dance to end they all said how much they had enjoyed their evening together. As they were all on the same floor and their rooms were near to each other, they went in the lift together and then said goodnight.

David took off his jacket, put it on a hanger and hung it up inside his wardrobe. He then went to the drinks cabinet, poured himself a nightcap, and was just about to sit down and enjoy his drink before getting ready for bed when the phone rang. Answering the phone he was somewhat surprised to hear Rosa's voice.

'Can I come to see you?' she asked. 'That is if you have not already retired to bed.'

'Of course you can come,' he replied. 'Would you like me to pour you a drink?'

Within a few minutes there was a tap at the door and Rosa entered. She was wearing a beautiful negligee and nightdress in red, with matching mule slippers. With a sly smile she said, 'I hear you like me to wear red.'

In her hand she held a small miniature china model of

Father Christmas. Holding it out to David she said, 'Father Christmas has brought you a present, if you would like to accept it, it is me and my love.'

Taking her in his arms, he kissed her on the mouth. When the kiss ended, Rosa said, 'Do you know, that is the first time that you have really kissed me. Now I know what I have been missing all these years.'

When David caught his breath from the surprise of her being there, he said, 'I guess I have loved you since the first time I saw you, and I've always been too scared to tell you so. As for wanting you for my Christmas present, I'm sure you know the answer without me having to tell you.'

Rosa took David by the hand and dropped the latch on the door, walked him across the room and lay beside him on the bed. Much later when Rosa was laid in David's arms she said, 'Are you satisfied with Father Christmas' present?'

'More than satisfied,' he answered. 'My Rosa, I never dreamed that I would enjoy anything so much, thank you. If Father Christmas realised what he was giving away he would have kept you for himself.'

'I loved it just as much as you, my David, for you are my David. You and Nancy are so very lucky in each having two people who love you so much. Ted and you loving her, and she and I loving you, but at least she has never made love to you as I have done tonight, and for that I am not jealous of her.'

Neither slept much that night, and they must have lost count of how many times they kissed each other as they lay in bed together. Rosa told David that in the New Year she would have to honour the engagements that she had, and would be on tour for a considerable amount of time. She told him that music played a great part in her life right now, that it gave her a very good lifestyle, also she had Maria and Abe to consider as they were her family and would always remain so. As she sat up in bed she turned, pulled down the shoulder straps on her nightdress and let it fall down, when David saw the scars on her back and body he said, 'Oh Rosa how you must have suffered, I never knew that anything had happened to you like that.'

'Now you know why I still have my tattoo,' she answered, 'the beatings were bad enough, but the worst thing was the electric treatments, which has deprived me from ever having children.'

Taking her in his arms, he held her so close to him and for almost the first time since being a child tears ran down his cheeks and on to her shoulders. Putting the straps back onto her shoulders, she wiped the tears from his face. 'Stop that,' she said with a smile, 'you'll spoil my new nightdress, and soldiers don't cry.'

'They do when they have seen and heard what I have just seen, and anyway I am not a solider now. Considering what you have been through I think that you are wonderful, and I can't express my feelings for you, I feel as though I want to hold on to you and never let go of you not even for a moment.'

'You will soon have to let me go, so I can return to my own room before the staff are on the move. We must not have your reputation damaged must we? Also like you I have a reputation to protect, and these days it is not easy with so much news, gossip and scandal, which fills the newspapers. You have told me so little of your life since we met, you seem to be living here at this hotel which must be quite expensive. I know how expensive hotels and cars can be, but you seem to have quite an influence here in this place.'

'Before too long I will tell you everything about myself, since the day we first met, up to the present time. But at the moment, I just want to hold you and kiss you until you go,' answered David.

Before they parted, David said that he had something very important to ask her, and that she had to think it over and give him an answer before the end of the Christmas holiday. 'Will you marry me?' he said.

'I will give you an answer before the holiday ends,' she answered, 'but now I must return to my own room. Merry Christmas my love,' she said, giving him a long drawn out kiss before leaving.

When Rosa returned to her room she lay under the bed covers, and although it was late, sleep did not come easy to her. Things seemed to go over and over in her mind, and before she did eventually fall asleep, she knew the answer she had to give to David and her cheeks were wet with tears, no doubt she cried herself to sleep, holding on to her St Christopher medallion, which hung around her neck.

The next morning the four of them met for breakfast and as it was a beautiful day they all went for a walk through the streets of London. David and Rosa walked hand in hand, as did Abe and Maria. Maria said it reminded her of long ago when she and Abe were much younger.

That evening there was a party in the hotel, which seemed to round the day off perfectly. Before they retired for the evening, David said that as it was Boxing Day tomorrow he would like to take them for a ride in the country if they wished.

Once again the weather was fine and they had a lovely day together, enjoying each other's company. They were back to the hotel in time to take their evening meal, and at the end of the evening the Christmas break was over. Before they said their goodbyes for the evening, David said that he was taking one or two more days off work, and that he would like to take Rosa back to the home town where they had grown up together, as there was something he wanted to show her. He hoped that Abe and Maria did not mind Rosa being away for a little while, and that he would take good care of her. They said that they did not mind, because they knew that Rosa was in good hands. Maria and Abe thanked David for a most wonderful Christmas, and said that it was the nicest Christmas that they had spent in years.

Rosa was up early the next day, practiced her violin, as she had neglected it for a day or two, and picked up her case that she had packed the previous night so as not to keep David waiting. After breakfast they said their goodbyes and were on their way to the old seaport. David's car was large and very comfortable to travel in and both enjoyed the ride. They talked throughout the journey, yet neither spoke of marriage, this was one subject that Rosa was avoiding.

As they entered the outskirts of the old town, both agreed that things did not appear to have changed a great deal. Riding around in the car was much easier and quicker than in the old days when they used to walk, or in David's case cycle. He parked the car and they walked off to find all their old haunts, they even remembered the spot where the dog had held Rosa against the wall. Here Rosa took David's hand, gave it a squeeze and said. 'Thanks David.'

David found his old shop, and then Mr Levine's shop; both had now changed, as had most things and most people. When David took her to the old hall where he had seen the people dancing for the first time it too had changed, or so it seemed to him. Turning to Rosa he said, 'When we find the right site I will build a house for us, as grand as this one used to be, only larger and more elegant.'

They were alone standing at the end of the drive leading to the hall when Rosa turned to David and said, 'Remember what my Papa said many years ago? "Oil and water. Oil and water never mix," and he meant you and I David. Today I am giving you my answer, and it is no. I cannot marry you. It is not that I don't love you; I could never love anyone as I love you. Please hear me out and please, please don't be angry with me.'

It was then that she said that there were too many obstacles in their way, that she was a Jewess and he a gentile, and there was Abe and Maria, and her music which meant so much to her. The travelling meant that she would be away from home for a good part of the year, but the main thing was that she could never give him a family, and if ever a man deserved a family of his own to love, it was he. If he wished, whenever possible, she would share his home and his bed with him, but if he was ever to fall in love with someone in the near future, she would disappear from his life forever, and then she would just be a memory. Turning towards him and looking up into his face with tears streaming down her face, David pulled her towards him saying, 'Angry with you, I will never be angry with you my love. If that is how you feel then so be it, but I will still build that house for us, when we find the right spot. I will always look forward to your coming home to me after each of your tours. You can bring Maria and Abe, for my home can be theirs as well as yours, and then you won't have to leave my bed in the middle of the night, as the house will be ours.'

Before they walked back to the car David held Rosa very close to him and said, 'Your Papa also said something else besides oil and water. He said, "Never try to hold a rainbow." Well I often hold on to a rainbow, in fact I am holding on to one right now, it is here in my arms, and when I had Father Christmas' present on Christmas Eve, never was a rainbow so perfect or so bright. So you see I am going to hold on to my rainbow,' and with that he wiped her tears and gave her a huge kiss.

* * * * *

After twelfth night, when Nancy and Ted were taking down the Christmas cards, Ted opened the one from David. Inside it he had written "Had an early Christmas present and a late one; the late one Father Christmas brought, was Rosa, my Jewess."

Turning to Nancy he said, 'I wonder what his early one was?'

Turning her face away from Ted, which now had a broad smile, she said, 'I wonder too, but I doubt if you will ever know.'